Man and Dog

Man AND Dog

BRAD STEIGER

DONALD I. FINE, INC.
New York

Copyright © 1995 by Brad Steiger

All rights reserved, including the right of reproduction in whole or in part in any form. Published in the United States of America by Donald I. Fine, Inc. and in Canada by General Publishing Company Limited.

Library of Congress Catalogue Card Number: 94-061906

ISBN: 1-55611-443-5

Manufactured in the United States of America

10 9 8 7 6 5 4 3 2 1

Designed by Irving Perkins Associates

Contents

ONE:	The Ancient Contract Between Dogs and Humans	1
TWO:	Queen—The Wild Dog Who Loved Us	6
THREE:	Talking with Dogs and Learning Their Idiosyncrasies	17
FOUR:	Canines as Symbols of Life's Mysteries	27
FIVE:	Penelope Smith Tells Us Who Animals Really Are	34
SIX:	Remarkable Reb, Beagle Extraordinary	39
SEVEN:	The Caretakers	45
EIGHT:	Medical Science Agrees: Dogs Are Good for Your Health!	55
NINE:	Eerie Footsteps on the Stairs for Queen, Reb, and Rascal	64
TEN:	Telepathically Locating a Missing Dog	77
ELEVEN:	Learning to Communicate with Your Dog	103
TWELVE:	Ghost Dogs—Do They Prove Survival?	129
THIRTEEN:	One Brief Moment in Time—Seven Wonderful Years with Sheila	140
FOURTEEN:	"Fred Is Waiting for Us in Heaven"	147
FIFTEEN:	Saying Hello to Toby Again—In Joey's Body	152
SIXTEEN:	The Weird and Wonderful World of Dogs	158
SEVENTEEN:	The Guardians	171
EIGHTEEN:	We Know Dogs Go to Heaven, Because They're Angels in Disguise	183
	References and Resources	197

ONE

The Ancient Contract Between Dogs and Humans

In his book *The Natural History of Nonsense,* author-educator Bergan Evans has a bit of fun with us dog lovers.

It is almost impossible, he suggests, to pass an evening in a group of ordinary, middle-class men and women without hearing of some example of a dog's supernatural powers. And if one should express a certain skepticism and attempt even the gentlest cross-examination of an avowed witness to a stupendous canine feat, that disrespectful heretic is immediately made to feel the fire of disapprobation from the defenders of the faith in doggy miracles.

"Dogs are sacred in our culture," Evans writes, "and nothing about them is more sacred than their ability to foretell the future, to warn of impending calamities, and to sense 'instinctively' the death of a master or a mistress who may chance at that moment to be far away."

I try always to maintain a good sense of humor—even when I am the butt of someone's joke. But since I am a firm believer in doggy miracles as well as in a spiritual connection between humans and canines, I often find myself becoming a bit impatient with those of my fellow two-leggeds who just don't seem to get it—who just don't seem to be able to appreciate the beautiful act of bonding with our best friend among all the multitude of animal species.

* * *

It may well be as simple as Scott Smith, author of *Pet Souls,* says, when in a recent letter to me he dissected the barrier of misunderstanding which exists between pet lovers and the rest of humankind:

> There are two kinds of people in the world—those who are pet lovers and those who aren't. The latter cannot understand why the former lavish so much money and attention on their pets. That is simply because those who think of animals as "things" have never bonded with a pet's personality and do not understand that it is no different from bonding with a human being. Pets are like young children—their incapacities and vulnerabilities make them more, not less, endearing.
>
> Some people feel threatened by the notion that animals are more than biological machines, for that implies that we should radically change the way we treat them. I think that as society evolves, we will increasingly come to recognize animals as sovereign souls worthy of respect and peaceful coexistence. Given that human beings are such a tiny fraction of animal life on this planet, anything that promotes such a goal is of tremendous importance. I believe that interspecies communication, both scientific and psychic, will be the key to our coming down off our arrogant pedestal.

One common characteristic that I have noticed in dog owners throughout the world is the fact that they usually become so attached to their dogs that they come to think of them as humans—or as equal entities—and consciously or unconsciously attribute to them human characteristics. For the dog owners who have bonded with their animals, there is no barrier to communication and there are few distinctions which exist to separate the canine mental processes from the human faculty of rational thought.

Penelope Smith, a unique specialist in interspecies communication, rejoices in the discoveries made by recent scientific investigations into the nature of animal intelligence which credit animals with having their own complex languages, emotions, and thought processes.

"Animals are intelligent beings with their own special awareness and wisdom, and many humans can learn to communicate with them directly," she says in her book, *Animals . . . Our Return to Wholeness*. "There is a growing realization, an awakening cultural awareness, that we are all linked—physically, mentally, and spiritually."

In my opinion, the contract that exists between dogs and humans constitutes history's longest-running unbroken agreement.

For years now, I have visualized the following little vignette from the dim, gray mists of prehistory.

It is anywhere from 12,000 to 20,000 years ago. An intelligent, essentially pragmatic, and especially hungry wolf stands just outside the ring of a campfire's light on a particularly dark, wet, and cold night. He catches the sour scent of humans, and he knows the fear of fire, but he also inhales the wonderful smell of meat cooking over the glowing coals.

He considers the situation: "All right, this is the way I see it. The hairy two-leggeds are slow, weak, and clumsy. They have no claws, and their teeth are not nearly long enough or sharp enough to cause great hurt to anything.

"But somehow they have won the awesome magic of fire, and they also possess the remarkable ability to pick up rocks and sticks with their front paws and throw them with great accuracy.

"They make sounds which appear somehow meaningful to others of their kind, and they very often work together as if they were one body and one mind. When they do this, they can conquer the greatest and most fierce of all creatures.

"They gather in packs, as we wolves do. They have family units, as we do. I sense somehow that we are brothers and sisters on some level of spirit. I sense that I can get along better with the two-legged ones than I could with any of the other four-legged or winged ones of the forest.

"Because I possess skills and abilities which the two-leggeds lack—and because I am well-known for my loyalty to the pack—I feel strongly that we can work out a really effective symbiotic relationship. And . . . and . . .

"Oh, my! Does that meat cooking over the coals ever smell delicious! Hey, you two-leggeds! Can we talk?"

Although I may have taken considerable literary license with the intelligent, pragmatic, and hungry wolf's interior monologue, I think that it was in some such manner that a remarkable social and spiritual contract was established between human and canine which has lasted unbroken for thousands of years. Somewhere along the pathway of evolutionary development for both species, the canines bade farewell to the kingdom of their fellow four-leggeds and threw in their lot with *Homo sapiens*. In a very real sense, I believe that dogs have become a kind of in-between species—less than human, but more than animal.

Later in this book, I will share details of my relationship with Queen, the offspring of a wild dog, which gave me the priceless opportunity to observe on a microcosmic level how early humans and canines might have come to an understanding born of mutual respect and a system of communication born of mutual need.

In addition to Queen, the aristocratic lady of the forest, I have walked together with Toby, a feisty little rat terrier; Rex, a stalwart shepherd; Bill, a loyal collie; Reb, a remarkably intelligent and stout fellow of a beagle; Trina, another wild dog we saved from death by entrapment in a pit; and Moses, our present four-legged companion, a powerful, perceptive, and good-natured black Labrador. All of these wonderful friends have in their own ways—and according to the marvelous idiosyncrasies of their own individual personalities—proved to be loyal, loving, and amazingly complex entities who have enormously enriched my lifewalk. Since earliest childhood, I have remained steadfastly convinced that the world was made a much better place for me because of the presence of a dog in my life—and I have never been long without a canine companion at my side.

Perhaps it is because of some remarkably benevolent Divine Plan that our species was first brought together with our four-legged brothers and sisters. Alas, the last ten thousand years or so have sadly demonstrated that we were not given these loyal and loving friends because we earned or deserved them. It has become steadily clearer to me that our canine companions are gifts from a loving God who blessed the human species with these devoted friends when it became obvious from our earliest days as sentient and upright beings that we needed all the help that we could get in order to survive on planet Earth.

I have also come to believe that we truly do have a soul connection between ourselves and our dogs, which on occasion allows us to blend energies and strengths in order to achieve new and even more important evolutionary goals. Dogs may act as a kind of conduit which enables us with their aid to achieve so much more than we might if left to our own physical devices alone and unassisted.

In my forty years of research into the paranormal, the metaphysical, and the unknown, I have even collected numerous accounts of instances in which it appears that angelic beings, higher intelligences, have been able temporarily to enter dogs and to accomplish miracles through their physical vehicles. As you will see later in this book, I am by no means alone in having reached such conclusions.

And of course I am by no means alone in my love of dogs. The latest statistics reveal that 36.3 million households—that's nearly forty percent of all homes in America—share room and board with a dog. And with four hundred breeds of dogs from which to choose, Americans have chosen 53 million canines to be their companions, playmates, protectors, guardians, burglar alarms, hunters, and fellow couch potatoes.

TWO

Queen—The Wild Dog Who Loved Us

In the spring of 1945, a terrible plague of distemper struck the dogs in northwestern Iowa.

We were a farm family that tilled 280 acres of corn, hay, oats, and soybeans, shepherded fifty head of cattle, about two hundred pigs, and a hundred or so chickens—and we desperately required the services of a good dog.

Old Bill, our stalwart collie, had finally succumbed to old age. Toby, our feisty little rat terrier, and big Rex, our sturdy shepherd, had both made the fatal mistake of being in the wrong place at the wrong time when a tractor suddenly shifted into reverse. And then the ugly disease had taken little Sport, a terrier pup we had barely had time to name, and we found ourselves without a dog.

Farmers in those days had to have a dependable four-legged troubleshooter to keep things running smoothly. Even if they could afford a decent, hardworking, two-legged hired hand to help with the seeding, cultivating, and harvesting of the field crops, farmers still needed to have a loyal dog to herd livestock and to bring the cows home for evening milking. After dark, when the bone-weary farmers were getting their sleep, their dreams were made more peaceful by the knowledge that their alert dog was standing watch, keeping foxes and civet cats away from the chicken house, discouraging raccoons from stealing the corn, and dissuading wild dogs from molesting the calves and small pigs.

Just a few months before, there had been no shortage of folks trying to give puppies away at county fairs, at gas stations, outside of grocery stores on Saturday nights. Now dogs were suddenly as scarce as white crows—and as valuable as gold nuggets.

We looked through the classified ads in the farm magazines that offered purebred dogs for sale, blue-blooded canines from fancy kennels with ritzy-sounding names. We knew that there was no way that we could afford to pay the kind of money that we suspected a professional dog breeder would want for "Glorious Mountain King III" or "Morgan's Martha IV" with their pedigrees. We wanted the kind of trustworthy mixed-breed mutt that we had always had. And we wanted one we could get for free.

One day a farmer, who supplemented his income by trapping mink, muskrats, and foxes along a creek that ran through a thick stand of woods, told us that he had first come upon a wild collie and her litter of pups about a month before. When he had sighted them recently, there was only one pup remaining.

"If you folks really need a dog so bad, you might try catching the wild bitch's pup before someone pops the both of them," he said to my dad one day at the farmer's elevator in town. "Trappers would rather shoot a wild dog than look at it, and the farmers in these parts will do the same. They lose too much livestock to foxes as it is. So if you want the pup that's left, you'd better hurry before someone nails 'im."

That night at the supper table, Dad brought up the matter of the wild pup for family discussion.

Even today, fifty years later, whenever we talk about Queen, Mom's recollection remains consistent: "She was a wild dog, part wolf. Both Dad and I saw the father slinking off in the distance when we got her. And we know he visited our farm many times, checking up on his pup. Wolves form family units, you know. They mate for life.

"Queen may have been a wild dog, but she was also the most human and the most intelligent dog we ever had."

Under ordinary circumstances, farmers like us would never have considered bringing a wild dog into our family circle. In fact, we probably would have shunned a wild dog even more than a fox, coyote, or wolf, because a dog that has broken free to run wild on its own will be smarter and meaner and more destructive than any creature that has never been domesticated.

Foxes, coyotes, or wolves kill only what they need to survive, and they usually single out only the old and the crippled from a herd of deer, moose, cattle, or sheep. But wild dogs often kill only for the fun of it, the sport of it—perhaps not unlike the human masters from whom they have fled—and they may leave twenty or more slaughtered sheep or a dozen mutilated cattle for a horrified farmer to discover during morning chores.

Dad presented other arguments against our attempting to corral the wild pup.

"It's a female. That means it will have pups. And we don't know for how many generations its mother's line has been wild. With a wolf for a father and a wild dog for a mother, she might just be impossible to tame. We might be bringing a killer home to watch our livestock.

"Another thing, some farmers who have seen the pup say that it is four to six months old. If you're going to have a dog turn out right, you have to get it as young as possible. This pup has already been raiding henhouses and running down sheep and cattle. It might already be too set in its ways to ever stop killing livestock."

The discussion went on past the farm news on radio station WHO from Des Moines.

I was nine years old, and Dad's mother, Grandma Dina, the town librarian, had read romantic tales of loyal dogs and enchanted beings to me since earliest childhood. I had a sure, romantic concept of our ability to soothe any savage impulses that might exist in any wild creature.

My sister June, who was still a few months from five years old, was only certain of one thing: she wanted a doggy to add to our menagerie of tame cats, cattle, pigs, chickens, ducks, and geese.

With the full understanding that we might never be able to domesticate fully the offspring of a wild dog, the next afternoon, just before chore time, the four of us set off for the section of the woods where the trappers and farmers had most often seen the outlaw collie and her pup.

We were joined at the edge of the forested area by the trapper and a neighboring farmer, who intended to kill the mother.

"I have no problem with you folks catching the pup and taking it home with you," the farmer said. "But," he added, nodding toward the .22 slide-action Winchester rifle he cradled in his left arm, "I mean to put an end to that mother dog's career of eating my chickens and my eggs."

The trapper said that he would help us try to run down the dogs. The farmer declined the exercise. He would wait near one of his outbuildings and try to get a shot at the mother dog if they tried to cut across his stockyard.

"Don't hit the pup," I admonished him.

The farmer laughed and reminded me that it was he who had won the American Legion annual trapshoot that fall. "I only hit what I aim at," he grinned.

Although we tried our best to be as quiet as possible in our approach to the wild dogs' lair, the big white collie emerged from their hiding place and watched us cautiously as we approached her turf.

Dad picked up a stout stick in case the collie's maternal instincts forced her to attack us.

She barked a couple of high-pitched warning yelps, and her pup crawled out from a dug-out area under a fallen tree. While the mother had a number of brown-colored patches in her white coat, the pup was all white except for her two black ears. They were both beautiful, magnificent creatures as they studied us, the unwelcome invaders of their wooded kingdom.

Dad was sizing up our prospective dog. "She's basically white collie, like the mother. Father was probably a shepherd, like Rex."

"You can see it's got wolf in it," Mom said, certain of her own expertise in assessing the qualities of a dog.

We got within about twenty yards of them, and then the dogs made their move. Instead of charging us, mother and pup set off running.

"Let's get them!" Dad shouted. "Run them down!"

In those days, my father was a man of considerable muscle, bulk, and—so it seemed from my nine-year-old perspective—nearly supernatural powers of endurance. As a high school athlete, he had won a trunkful of medals and trophies in the shot put and the discus throw. He had lettered in baseball and basketball. At twenty-one, he had been set to live his dream as a professional baseball player when he was beaned by a fastball during the final cut and had to be hospitalized for a skull fracture rather than taking the bus to baseball camp.

But in spite of his impressive athletic prowess, Dad was not a runner, so when he gave the order to "run them down," he was shouting primarily to his fleet-footed wife, a woman who had always been a sports-loving tomboy and who especially loved to run.

The hefty trapper, even bulkier than Dad, together with my short, stocky legs and June's five-year-old enthusiasm, would have to do the best we could to keep up with Mom.

I still don't know how we did it, but after what proved to be an endurance race through the woods, our winded, panting group somehow managed to win our prize when we cornered the snarling pup against an old rusted wire fence. Although a mother dog will fight to the death to defend her young pups, this Mama must have considered her offspring old enough to fend for itself, because she kept right on running without looking back to determine its fate.

We heard shots a few minutes later, but the farmer waiting by his stockyard missed her on that afternoon. Apparently fast-moving collies were harder targets to hit than the clay pigeons at the annual American Legion trapshoot. A couple of days later, though, we were told that he shot and killed the white collie in his barn when he caught her in the act of eating one of his plumpest Leghorn roosters.

Dad pulled on thick leather work gloves, then took off his belt and looped it around the dog's snapping jaws. None of us wanted to be bitten—especially by a dog that had never had rabies or distemper shots.

We took a few minutes to catch our breath and to inspect our newly acquired canine farmhand.

Dad was not all that pleased. The female collie-shepherd mix appeared to be even older than our trapper friend had estimated.

"Yep," the trapper agreed. "She could be six months or better. She might just have enjoyed a little too much of the wild and free life to ever settle down for you."

"You can sure tell she has wolf in her," Mom repeated her earlier assessment.

Dad laughed wryly and shook his head. "We'll probably never be able to train or domesticate her. And she'll probably eat our chickens and kill our pigs."

But after several minutes of serious deliberation concerning the young female dog's ultimate destiny, we decided that our desperate need for a dog surpassed all other considerations and circumvented all negative eventualities. We thanked our trapper friend for his help, then we wrapped the snarling, struggling dog in the Indian blanket that we always kept in the back seat of our old Chevy, and we carried her with us to our farm.

I don't think we ever thought of calling her anything other than Queen. With her haughty, imperious, no-nonsense manner, she proved to be one of the most incredibly rich and complex personalities that I have ever known. She will always remain in my memory as an entity who was as individual and as unique as any human being with whom I have become friends and shared deep and meaningful experiences.

In fact, as I grow older, I am even more able to appreciate the full impact of the marvelous opportunity that my family was given to be able to share our rough farm life with a four-legged, sovereign entity who always demanded that she be accepted as an equal on her own terms—and yet who came to give of herself unselfishly and completely.

In the years to come, Queen worked with us, nearly froze to death in blizzards with us, defended us, and loved us without holding back an iota of her energy.

But never as "just a pet," never as "only a dog." Always as Queen, an individual, independent being, who was our friend, our partner, our co-worker, our full-fledged family member.

The first week or so was terrible. We had to keep her locked in the cobhouse, the old building near the house in which we kept the corncobs we used in our cookstove.

She was vicious. It seemed as though she never stopped snarling, snapping.

For days she wouldn't eat, and to try to coax her to take a bite of food was interpreted by Queen as an invitation to take a bite out of your hand.

June cried. She wanted to play with our new puppy. She thought Dad was being mean, keeping her locked up in the cobhouse.

Although Dad explained that Queen would run away, back to the woods and back to the wild, unless we kept her locked up, June still thought it was cruel to keep her cooped with the cobs and the mice.

I, too, was impatient to romp and play with our new dog. I began to think it was a hopeless task. It was beginning to seem as though we should have left her in the woods. She would never become tame enough even to pet.

And then, whether it was starvation or common sense that

got the better of her, Queen began to accept the food that we offered her.

For weeks thereafter, it was still one step at a time. I received a painful bite to my fingers when I tried to pet her before she was ready to receive a touch from any of us.

One of the first major breakthroughs came with Queen's dog license and collar. We had had her for about six weeks, and it appeared as though she would become domesticated enough to serve as our four-legged farmhand. If we were going to keep her—and we had voted unanimously to do so—we would have to license her to distinguish her from the packs of stray and wild dogs that were anathema to farmers and their livestock.

Queen had come to appreciate regular meals, and she would endure a friendly pat or scratch every now and then. It was not yet possible to embark on any meaningful training session with her, for she would not tolerate any form of correction or criticism. To attempt to scold Queen for a misdeed or an inability to follow a command was only to prompt a snarl and a warning growl in return.

When Dad first approached her with the collar that bore a metal dog license and a few ornamental metallic studs, Queen showed her teeth and backed off.

"Queen," Dad promised in a cheerfully enthusiastic voice, "you'll look pretty. It's your spiffy new collar. Oh, see how pretty it is!"

Although I was only nine, I looked at my father in wonderment. How could he think that a dog—a wild one at that—would understand the concept of prettiness? And while we might grant the ancient stereotype of female vanity some people base on personal observation of the ladies of our species, how could Dad think that a female dog would be at all interested in looking pretty?

"Come on, kids," Dad encouraged June and me. "Tell Queen how pretty the collar is. Tell her how spiffy she'll look when she wears it."

If our big, burly father could flatter a dog without embarrassment, what did we have to lose? We joined his chorus of seduction and began to sing the praises of the magnificent leather collar.

Strangely enough, Queen seemed interested in giving her new look a try. To my astonishment, she ceased her snarling and permitted Dad to fasten the collar around her neck.

Oh, boy, I thought. Here we go! The minute she feels the tightness of leather around her throat, she is going to go crazy. She will snap and snarl and tear through the yard until she somehow manages to rip the noose from her neck.

It never happened. Queen actually seemed to preen, to strut back and forth in front of us.

"Look how pretty she is!" Dad said with all the excitement of a prospector stumbling upon a gold mine. "Look at Queen's spiffy new collar!"

From that day on, it was impossible to touch that collar under any circumstances. To remove it in order to trim her hair in the hot and humid Iowa summers was out of the question. Even playfully suggesting that one might want to borrow her collar or try it on would invite a warning growl. If one persisted in expressing a lust for the collar and made a move toward it, one could expect a painful nip that was designed to alter such designs once and for all.

Reflecting upon the experience fifty years later, I cannot believe that Queen had yet had enough time to comprehend human notions of "pretty" and "spiffy." Since I have now had subsequent interactions with other dogs that have demonstrated to my satisfaction that on occasion our canine companions might truly understand nearly everything we say to them or to each other, I would not doubt that Queen could have perceived precisely what we were talking about, had she had enough time to learn our language, so to speak. Since she had been a member of our family for such a short period of time when the collar incident occurred, I am much more inclined to believe that she picked up our mental images of her wearing the collar, heard our cheerful voices underscoring the visual impressions, and decided that it would indeed be a good thing to wear such an object around her neck. And perhaps she did have just a bit of personal vanity about her appearance that extended beyond the perimeters of the typical canine devotion to her own tail.

In many ways, having Queen around was like being in the presence of an austere, humorless aunt who tirelessly insisted upon proper behavior at all times. Queen never permitted any kind of roughhousing, and she seldom allowed herself to engage in any sort of playful activity.

If Mom and Dad were to tussle affectionately with one another, they would each receive a nip from Queen in reprimand that they were to stick to the serious business of getting in the crops.

If either or both of us kids were to tussle affectionately with Mom or Dad, all three or four of us would receive the nip of negation from the no-nonsense collie.

And, of course, woe unto any friends of ours who might come over to play with us on days when we didn't have to work in the fields. Sometimes our only recourse was to trick Queen into following us into the barn—and then locking her in! If she somehow managed to escape, however, it would be woe unto all of us for tricking her; she would nip us one by one.

June and I found that Queen's general grumpiness constituted a challenge to create a game that she *would* play with us. We would wait until she was napping peacefully, then we would sneak up on her and throw an old blanket over her sleeping form.

The rules of this crude game were simple: Try to wrap Queen up so well that by the time she got free we could be safely inside the house or barn before we got nipped.

We seldom made it to safety before we each got a nasty nip as punishment for our impudence in disturbing her nap. And even when we did manage to get inside the house or barn before she got free, she would be waiting for us when we finally emerged. Once we discovered that it mattered not to Queen if she had to wait two or three hours before delivering the nip of retribution, the fun quotient of the wrap-Queen-in-a-blanket game began to diminish.

It would not be fair to say that Queen *never* played a game with us. She did enjoy one bizarre play activity that was somehow mysteriously set in motion by Mom's singing and dancing with us.

Whenever Mom would take us by our hands, start to sing in her delightfully unique blend of French and Danish lyrics, and commence to dance with us in a circle, Queen would begin to run in her own ever-narrowing circles. Sometimes she would begin running in circles that were easily thirty yards or more in circumference. She would run at full speed, slowly, steadily, decreasing the circle's size until she connected with our own circle dance with such velocity that she would send the three of us sprawling on impact.

Wild dogs play rough.

THREE

Talking with Dogs and Learning Their Idiosyncrasies

The more I thought about my father convincing a snarling wild dog barely out of the woods to let him place a collar around her neck, the more I was intrigued by the process of interspecies communication that must have been involved in the sudden achievement of such a high level of understanding and trust.

And the fact that it had been my always pleasant but very taciturn, down-to-earth, practical father who had been the one who had cajoled Queen into compliance was even more intriguing.

According to her family's tradition, my mother was related to the famous Danish storyteller, Hans Christian Andersen. I don't know whether or not that claim was ever authenticated, but I do know for a fact that Mom's imagination and her marvelous bedtime stories easily matched Hans' tales of little mermaids and thumb-sized dancing girls.

But it had been Dad who had made this fascinating mental linkup with our still very wild and untamed dog.

I began to notice that each morning upon leaving the house to do chores, Dad acted as though he were genuinely glad to see Queen. He told her how good she was and what a fine job she had done keeping away creatures of darkness while we had slept.

And believe it or not, he also sang to her. This big, rugged man sang to his dog.

Although my father never claimed to have a good singing voice, he refused to let such a minor impediment stand in the way of his bursting into song whenever the spirit so moved him. And each of the "Queen songs"—whether they were spontaneous parodies of current favorites or his unique, updated renditions of folk classics—incorporated her name somehow into the lyrics.

Perhaps there is truth after all to the saying that "Music hath charm to soothe the savage beast." I know that I have followed my father's practice of singing to each of my subsequent dogs.

My beagle Reb had his morning greeting song and a special theme song that I would sing out whenever he entered the room. Moses, our current companion, has a song for his walk, another for his nighttime treat, still another for bedtime, and so on. Sherry, my wife, soon picked up the habit; and Moses needs to hear only a few of the opening notes of each to respond with the appropriate behavior.

I also noticed that Dad spoke to Queen as if she were truly a human hired hand and he fully expected her to conduct herself accordingly. Again, he would praise her extravagantly for the smallest deed done correctly, withholding affection only if she erred.

I began to see that the basic key to communication with Queen was to treat her with genuine affection. And as I came to analyze the situation in later years, I saw that such an expression of love was truly the most logical means of getting through to her or to any wild or unruly dog.

As an undomesticated dog, Queen seemed to be without fear of humans or anything else. When she was but a pup, even the largest of adversaries could not intimidate her. And to attempt to beat her into submission—besides being unconscionably cruel—would have been stupid and unproductive. Harsh and brutal treatment on our part would most likely have caused her only to run away or to grow steadily more vicious—or eventually to attack whoever was tormenting her.

Fifty years later, I remain convinced that love is the greatest power in the universe and that it works as effectively with animals as with humans. Each time I take Moses for our walk along the river, I continually project loving thoughts toward him, and my repeated intonation of "Good boy" becomes our mantra.

Don't we all like to hear that we are good boys or good girls? And don't we all do better for those who think of us as good, rather than bad?

I began to make a real point of carefully watching Queen's body language. Although I came to believe that she could understand nearly everything we said—and *thought*—I found that I could better comprehend her mental processes if I just took a few moments to observe her body stance or movements. I cannot claim that I was able to distinguish with unfailing accuracy which aspects of her body language were distinctly her own and which were universal vocabulary words in the doggy dictionary, but I have been able to use all of the following signs to "talk" to many, many dogs over the past five decades.

When Queen lifted a forepaw toward me, I decided that was akin to saying "May I have?" Or sometimes the gesture seemed to mean "Please pay attention to me."

When her ears were pricked up and her lips were raised around her teeth, she was telling me to back off. "Don't mess with me just now, please."

A soft lick on my hand translated as her telling me that she loved me.

If her ears were pulled back and she looked at me with soulful eyes, she was relaying her distress or unhappiness with a situation.

When she rolled over on her back and exposed her stomach, she was apologizing for having done something she knew upset or angered me.

On very rare occasions, Queen would hold her tail high and

wag it quite vigorously. She would lower her torso onto her forepaws and stick her rear end up and "smile" with her mouth open. I eventually learned that this was her sign that she was in a playful mood.

As I said, Queen seldom became playful, but our Labrador Moses goes into this stance whenever Sherry or I indicate that it **is** time for a walk or a drive. He usually follows this movement with a joyful jump from a squatting position.

If I came upon Queen lying stretched out in the sun on a chilly day and she looked up at me with eyes that were half-closed, I knew that she was indicating she was relaxed and wanted to catch some shut-eye. She would not respond favorably at that time to a suggestion that was not crucial to the general well-being of the entire farmstead.

If I persisted when she was intending to nap and her eyes moved from half-closed to very narrow slits, I soon learned that she was warning me to take a hike.

Should I continue to pester her beyond this point and her ears would suddenly rotate forward, I was being warned that she would happily bite my butt if I didn't leave her alone.

I also discovered that just because Queen might be wagging her tail she was not necessarily telling me that she was happy. Such a rapid movement of her tail could also mean that she was excited about something and might be uncertain how she should proceed.

Although I have since heard of fellows who claim their dogs love to guzzle beer, I noticed that Queen took an instant dislike to anyone with alcohol on his or her breath. This may have been accentuated by the fact that both of my parents were non-drinkers, as were most of our friends and relatives. Therefore, it would stand to reason that the scent of whiskey or a couple of cocktails would be quite alien to Queen's nostrils.

I observed Queen to act in a similar aggressive manner around cigarette, cigar, or pipe smokers. She simply did not like the smell of burning tobacco.

Again, neither of my parents smoked, and few among their

closest friends ever lighted up. Tobacco smoke could have been yet another signal to Queen that strangers were among us.

On the other hand, I soon perceived that the sense of smell was Queen's—or any dog's—most powerful faculty. It's obvious that they don't have a strong sense of taste or they couldn't eat some of the wretched things they dig up after a few months of decay. They don't see all that well and are probably color blind. And while their sense of hearing might be somewhat more sensitive than ours under certain conditions, it is easily confused or irritated by high-pitched frequencies, such as sirens, whistles, certain musical instruments, and squealing children.

Smell is definitely their sense—which is why a man can be torn to shreds by his faithful attack dog if he tries to enter the apartment wearing a new and different brand of cologne, a sport coat and a pair of trousers he borrowed from a friend, and dark glasses shading his eyes.

Queen always seemed to know before we did when a blizzard, electrical storm, or tornado was coming. When I was a boy, I was convinced that she truly had precognitive abilities that placed her far above the weather man on the radio. Now I am willing to concede that her ability to hear the high-pitched keening of the approaching winds may have had something to do with her prophetic prowess. I can remember her shaking her ears as if they were troubling her, causing her pain. In retrospect it might well have been the shrill sound of powerful winds rushing across the plains toward our farm that irritated her ears and forced her to seek shelter in advance of the approaching storm.

Queen was definitely a one-family dog, and it seemed clear that she also preferred our company to that of any other dog. Although she had herself been wild, she tirelessly drove off any stray dog or any roving packs of canine killers bent on slaughtering our livestock. Never a particularly large dog, Queen fearlessly attacked a single stray or a half dozen marauding mutts with equal impulsiveness.

One night when Dad was in town attending a meeting, Mom was awakened from her nap in front of the radio by the sounds of a terrible dogfight outside by the barn. Without hesitation, my fearless and impulsive mother went to investigate.

Queen was doing her best to keep five large dogs from entering the barn and going after some newborn calves. Two powerful German shepherds had her down when Mom charged into the fray, launching powerful kicks into the ribs and skulls of the massive dogs who were tearing at Queen's throat.

The invaders backed off long enough for Queen to get to her feet, and she and Mom started a desperate run for the house.

And then the angry German shepherds were blocking Mom's path, unwilling to let her escape.

But Queen had caught her second breath. She attacked the two much larger dogs with such fury that they went yelping away in painful retreat.

Mom held the door open for Queen, and the two of them entered the safety of our farmhouse.

When Dad returned home, he berated Mom for having charged out into the darkness and into the midst of a vicious dogfight.

Mom's reply was simple and direct. "I could tell from the sounds of things that Queen was getting the worst of it. I knew she was trying to defend the calves, and those wild dogs would probably kill her. I had to save her life. I got those monsters off her, and we ran for the house. Then Queen ended up saving my life. Those two big German shepherds would surely have got me down and ripped open my throat."

A few months later, it was Queen's latent wild nature that nearly got her killed.

She had her batch of pups far too young. She had become pregnant during her first season when she herself was little more than a pup.

When Queen delivered her four puppies, we were living on Uncle Frosty's place. We fixed up a place for her in the cobhouse and gave her some old blankets to snuggle into with her babies.

It was Saturday night, and that meant a trip to town and a chance to go to the movies. June and I were reluctant to leave Queen alone. She was still very weak from having just given birth, but Mom and Dad assured us that Queen had everything under control.

When we came home around eleven o'clock that night, we were startled to see Queen outside of the cobhouse, staggering as if from exhaustion.

"Whatever could make her leave her pups unattended?" Mom wanted to know.

"Maybe Queen isn't such a good mother," I suggested.

"Wait! Look!" Dad shouted. He had left on the car's headlights, and we were suddenly able to see another figure in the shadows.

In a blur of motion, something came running at Queen and knocked her sprawling.

Queen rolled back to her feet, emitting a pitiful whine. She caught at something dark and furry with her teeth, gave it a shake, and tossed it five or six feet away from her.

Whatever it was landed with a thud, and Queen braced herself for another onslaught.

"My gosh!" Dad said. "It's a big muskrat!"

"It's after her pups!" Mom said.

We could see now that there were splotches of blood on Queen's white coat where the muskrat had bitten her. The huge rodent had smelled the newborn puppies and the afterbirth and had come up from the creek to dine on fresh dog meat.

"Poor Queen," June was saying. She had fallen asleep in the backseat on the drive home from town and had awakened to the nightmarish scene. "We have to help her! The big rat wants to eat her babies!"

Dad was already on his way into the house to get the 12-gauge shotgun from the front porch.

Queen blocked another charge by the muskrat and yelped as its prominent front teeth tore at her flesh.

With an angry growl, Queen got her teeth behind the creature's neck, shook it violently several times, and threw it as far away from her as her fading strength would allow.

The muskrat landed once again with a heavy thud, but got quickly back on its feet. It was tough, mean, and determined to feast on fresh meat.

Queen's entire body was trembling with extreme fatigue as she braced herself for another charge.

Blam! The roar of the shotgun blasted the unwelcome invader into bloody bits of flesh, bone, and bristle.

Queen's ordeal was over. She collapsed, whimpering as her legs folded beneath her.

Then she struggled back to her feet and limped into the cobhouse to check on her babies.

Dad turned on the light in the shed. "They're all present and accounted for," he told us. "The muskrat didn't get any of Queen's pups."

From the looks of the grass in our yard, the deadly struggle between the new mother and the predator must have gone on for hours. Once again, Queen proved that she had courage and heart.

But it was when those pups for whom she had fought so valiantly were maturing that Queen's own wild side nearly caused Dad to use the shotgun on her.

"I found two more dead chickens," he said angrily one night at supper.

"Is it foxes?" Mom asked as she set the mashed potatoes on the table.

"It's Queen," Dad said in disgust.

"It can't be," I protested. "Queen wouldn't do such a thing."

"Must be foxes," June put in. "Can't be Queenie."

Dad shook his head. "It's Queen, all right. She's teaching her pups to hunt just like her mother taught her. She's showing them how to stalk game—only the game is our chickens!"

Mom looked disappointed. "She's reverting to the wild, to the wolf blood that's in her."

"We can't have it," Dad pronounced with finality. "Farm dogs can't be killers. Queen is supposed to protect our livestock, not eat it."

"She'll stop, Dad, I know she will," June promised, as if she had special insight into the problem. "I just know she will."

Dad nodded solemnly. "She'll stop it—or we'll have to get rid of her."

I lay awake half the night. I couldn't imagine life without Queen. But I had seen her stalking the chickens with my own eyes. She would get way down on her stomach and begin a crawl toward her prey. When she felt herself in position, she would charge a hen or rooster, snatch it in her jaws, and kill it with a quick snap of its neck. Once the demonstration was completed, she would indicate that it was one of her pups' turn.

I had seen it. I had kept quiet. I hadn't tattled on Queen, because I had hoped that she would stop it. I mean, how could she even pretend that a dumb old chicken was something that was meant to be stalked?

I fell asleep praying for a solution, and I awakened the next morning with an inspiration.

I got my Red Ryder bee-bee gun and did some stalking of my own. I found Queen just as she was going into her crawl and about to charge a chicken. Her four pups were close behind, watching their mother's every move.

I was completely hidden from the dogs' view as I crouched behind the lowest boughs of a large pine. I mentally asked Queen for forgiveness, then fired at her hindquarters.

Queen yelped sharply in surprise and pain as the bee-bee found its target. Then, suspecting the pup nearest her of being the perpetrator, she angrily rolled him over with her jaws, smartly biting him until his yelps of protest scared away the nearby chickens.

I kept this up for an entire morning and afternoon. There was no way that I was going to face the prospect of Dad having to do away with Queen.

Each time she would go into her crouch and begin to zero in on a feathered victim, I would let fly a bee-bee at her butt.

And each time the nearest pup would be mangled by an angry mama, who blamed him or her for the grossest sort of maternal disrespect.

Queen never saw me and I am certain never suspected that her loving little master would ever bruise her bottom; but by the end of the day, she had sworn off killing chickens for good. The conditioned response of a painful bee-bee in the hindquarters every time she began to stalk a hen or rooster had accomplished its purpose for both Queen and her pups.

From Queen's perspective, why should she teach such nasty, disrespectful children how to survive in the wilderness?

And the poor pups must have thought that the very sight of a chicken transformed their mother into a violent lunatic, who attacked them without any provocation.

Queen never killed another chicken or attacked any other of our livestock ever again. The final vestiges of her wild bloodlust had been drained by a series of well-aimed bee-bees.

FOUR

Canines as Symbols of Life's Mysteries

The entire canine contingent—wolves, coyotes, foxes, and dogs—figured very prominently in the lives of early humans, sometimes as gods, often as demons, always as predators, frequently as protectors. Take, for instance, the multiple roles that the canine family played in the evolution of the native people on the North American continent.

When I was adopted into the Wolf Clan of the Seneca, my adoptive mother, Twylah Nitsch, told me that it was from the wolf that the early people learned forethought before decision, the importance of family loyalty and unity, and the knowledge of a great deal of their medicine power.

The wolf was a sacred totem and clan symbol for many tribes throughout all of Europe, as well as North America. Many heroes on both sides of the Atlantic claimed ancestry from wolves.

A number of Native American tribes have it in their legends that the first men were created in the shape of wolves. At first they walked on all fours; then, slowly, they began to develop more human members—an occasional toe, a finger, an ear, an eye.

As time went by, they evolved two toes, three toes; more fingers; two eyes and ears.

Finally, by slow progression, they became perfect men and women.

Sadly, though, the practice of sitting upright eventually cost them their fine, bushy tails; but they could always take one from a fox or a wolf to attach to their breeches.

Some of the eastern tribes say that the Great Mystery gave the wolf the distasteful task of informing the animals which of their number were to be designated as food for humans. Brother Wolf instructed them that they should not resist but permit themselves to be slain, as long as the method of killing was a quick and merciful one.

The Navajo blame the wolf for scattering the stars across the night sky.

In the beginning, so the legend goes, the ancient wise men agreed that there should be more light on Earth. The Navajo were assigned the task of constructing a Sun, and various other tribes were given the job of creating the Moon and the stars.

Then the ancient wise men decided to give the Sun and the Moon to the supervision of two mute flute players, who have carried the two heavenly bodies ever since.

After the Sun and Moon had been hung, people from many tribes began to embroider the stars in the heavens in beautiful and varied patterns and images. Bears and fishes and all varieties of animals were being drawn—when in rushed a prairie wolf, who roughly exclaimed:

"What folly is this? Why are you making all this fuss to arrange the stars so perfectly in patterns? Just stick them anywhere!"

Suiting his actions to his words, the impatient wolf scattered a large pile of celestial sparklers all over the heavens—and that is how they remain to this day.

To the Dakota tribes, the spirit of the North, the bringer of ice and snow and freezing cold, was assisted in his chilly work by wolves.

Yet other tribes credit the wolf for having brought summer to Earth. In the beginning, when the people of Turtle Island (North

America) were not receiving enough warmth, it was only the wolf who could jump high enough to tear a hole in the sky and let the Sun's fire get through the canopy of clouds.

In the folklore of many tribes, the fox was often associated with sorcery and witchcraft, and its image was frequently used by witches as a vehicle into which they projected their spirits when they wished to travel in animal form.

The fox was also prized as a "familiar" by those practitioners of negative medicine power; and as in Europe, it became the symbol of wiliness, quick-wittedness, and a crafty kind of wisdom.

Contrary to the eternal bad luck of Wiley E. Coyote in the Warner Brothers Road Runner cartoons, in Native American lore it is Brother Coyote who almost always has the last laugh.

To some tribes, the coyote was an early savior of humankind. According to the legend, the Sun had nine blazing brothers, none of whom cared that their presence was scorching Mother Earth and roasting her children. Assessing the fiery situation and deducing its solution, the coyote slew the Sun's thoughtless brothers and rescued the tribespeople from their giant funeral pyre.

But humankind's collective fat was no sooner out of the frying pan than the Moon's nine sisters, each as cold and icy as she, elected to turn night into a freezing torment for the people of Mother Earth.

Well, it even got too cold for Brother Coyote, and the people despaired when they saw their champion trot off to the east.

But not to worry. He temporarily retreated to the far eastern edge of the world, devised how to create fire from flint so he could warm his paws, then he went after those frigid sisters and slew them one by one. Once again he had saved humankind from what had appeared to be an impossible situation and an ultimately dire outcome.

* * *

The coyote occupies a most unique place in the legends and folklore of the Native Americans, especially for the southwestern tribes. Although he is very often said to have been intimately associated with the Great Mystery in the very act of creation, his wily descendants are both pests and competitors in the tough business of survival in desert country.

According to legend, it was the coyote who gave the tribespeople the life-giving gift of fire. He is said to have taught the early people how to grind flour, and he showed them which herbs would bring about which cures.

But in spite of his many benevolent acts, Brother Coyote has a most peculiar temperament, and he remains forever a Trickster. While it was he who brought humankind fire, he is also credited for having brought Death into the world.

The majority of Native American tribes so revered Brother Dog that their legends stated that it was one of his kind who waited in the Way of Departed Spirits to assist a recently deceased soul in finding its way to the Land of the Grandparents.

Such reverence for our special four-legged friend was widely practiced among many nations. In ancient Egypt, Anubis, the dog or jackal-headed god, presided over the embalming of the dead and led the spirits of the deceased to the hall of judgment. In Persia, dogs were believed to be able to protect the soul from evil spirits; and when a person was dying, a dog was stationed by his or her bedside to keep away the evil spirits who hovered near newly released souls.

In addition to its role as a guide to the Other Side, many Native American tribes associated the dog with the sun and the moon. Certain folklorists have theorized that such an association may have been due to the dog's well-known penchant for howling at the moon on shadowy, moonlit nights.

The dog's connection to the sun may well have derived from what seems to be its instinctive habit of walking around in a small circle before it sits or lies down, and its custom of racing around in circles whenever it has any occasion to be happy or excited. To the early people, a circle was a symbol of the sun, thus ennobling the dog with high status.

The dog, in Grandmother Twylah's view, represents fidelity and devotion. The dog symbolizes a friend who is always available when he or she is truly needed.

Find Your Dog's Position on the Medicine Wheel

As long as we seem to be in a Native American vibration, you might find it interesting to see where your dog fits into the Medicine Wheel that was given to Sun Bear in a vision and perfected in material expression by his Medicine Helper Wabun Wind. The Medicine Wheel is a kind of Native American zodiac, and if you know the birth date of your dog, you might gain some insight into its personality from the totem animal that represents its sign.

March 21 to April 19: The Red Hawk. Dogs born under the sun sign of the Red Hawk are likely to be adventurous and assertive. They probably enjoy nothing more than an unfettered romp in the outdoors, and you may find that your Red Hawk dog becomes a bit stubborn and headstrong at times.

April 20 to May 20: The Beaver. Beaver dogs are generally blessed with good health and great powers of physical endurance. They are loyal and stable animals who prize their peace and security and who will do their best to protect yours.

May 21 to June 21: The Deer. Those dogs born under the sign of the Deer seem to be almost constantly in motion. It won't trouble Deer dogs if you should have to move occasionally, for they love change and the challenge of new environments.

June 22 to July 21: The Brown Flicker. If your dog was born under the sign of the Brown Flicker, you may have detected that he or she has a strong nesting instinct and takes great comfort in a stable homelife. If your dog is a female, she will make an exceptionally good mother to her litter.

July 22 to August 21: The Sturgeon. Although you find your Sturgeon dog compliant enough, you may have noticed that it usually demands that it be the dominant canine when it encounters other dogs. As the dog grows older, you may find that it will on occasion attempt to show you that it is the boss.

August 22 to September 22: The Bear. Your Bear dog is a no-nonsense canine who is very suspicious of strangers and who will not tolerate insincerity or deceit. It will usually be a cautious, quiet dog, somewhat slow-moving though always ready to comply with your wishes.

September 23 to October 22: The Raven. Adaptability is the keyword for your Raven dog. It is usually extremely flexible and adjusts very well to new environments and circumstances. You may, however, on occasion find it filled with a bit too much nervous energy.

October 23 to November 21: The Snake. A natural charmer, the dog born under the Medicine Wheel sign of the Snake is usually Mr. or Ms. Personality. You would be well-advised to give this somewhat highly strung dog a lot of love and attention.

November 22 to December 21: The Elk. The Elk Dog is most often very active and robust. You will find it competitive with, though seldom hostile to, other dogs. Those dogs born under this sign love to travel and to discover new areas of fields, meadows, and woods.

December 22 to January 20: The Snow Goose. Dogs born under the sign of the Snow Goose are hardworking, loyal, and dependable canines who make good hunters, watchdogs, and shepherds. You can best reward them by providing them with a stable homelife, for they do not adjust well to sudden changes in their routine.

January 21 to February 18: The Otter. Although those dogs born under the Medicine Wheel sign of the Otter can sometimes be unpredictable when you first acquire them as pups, they usually prove to be loyal and dependable friends as they mature. Exercise a little patience at the beginning of your relationship, and you will come to cherish a good-natured canine companion.

February 19 to March 20: The Cougar. Patience is also required in your initial interactions with the dog born under the sign of the Cougar. These dogs are often extremely sensitive and easily hurt by disapproval and rejection. Try to be understanding of this dog's emotional needs, and you will soon have perhaps the most obedient and loving canine you have ever encountered.

FIVE

Penelope Smith Tells Us Who Animals Really Are

Penelope Smith's avowed mission on planet Earth is to help people return to their innate ability to communicate telepathically with other species.

Why is this so important to her?

"So we don't destroy the planet. So we don't lose it all. Our culture has been geared for several hundred years to separating humans from the rest of nature. When we turned to industrialization, when we turned to the scientific approach of looking at other species as objects, we ended up losing the spiritual connection and divorcing ourselves from the rest of nature. It is our separation from other species and our use of them that has caused our decline and is leading to the destruction of our planet."

Practically every dog owner talks to his or her canine companion, but only a very few are willing to open their minds, lower the barriers of prejudiced thought, and listen to what their dogs may be saying back to them.

Penelope lives in Point Reyes, California, with her husband and business manager Michel Sherman, but she travels throughout the United States and abroad to conduct workshops on interspecies communication. Far from considering her talents special and unique, she believes that everyone is born with the ability to communicate telepathically with animals.

"This ability is carefully squeezed out of us when we are children," she observes sadly. "Telepathy is considered something weird or strange, but in actual fact, it is the universal language.

"I have communicated with animals all my life. First you have to learn how to quiet your mind. Once your mind is open and receptive, the images and impressions of what the animal is thinking and feeling will come through. All beings are quite capable of understanding another being without opening their mouths. The whole secret of what I do is to *listen* to them."

Penelope wishes that all humans would take the time to listen to their pets.

"Animals are usually overjoyed to meet a human being who communicates through thoughts and feelings instead of just observing their behavior."

When you first try to apply her admonition to listen and do your best to communicate with your dog, Penelope recommends that you keep things on a simple basis.

"Which is not to say that dogs are simple beings," she stresses. "Many of them have been around the block a few times and have many tales to tell. But it is important for people to clearly communicate their thoughts, intentions, and mental images so their dogs do not get confused."

You would be dead wrong if you decided to make a superficial characterization of Penelope Smith as a nature girl with a Saint Francis complex. She has earned bachelor's and master's degrees in the social sciences with experience in counseling. She is also well versed in the study of human nutrition, and she has done solid research in the areas of animal nutrition, anatomy, behavior, and care.

And she tries always to give practical advice.

In an interview in the September 1994 Psychic Reader, writer Caitlin Phillips admitted to a fear of dogs that stemmed from a childhood attack. Rather than pompously scolding Ms. Phillips for harboring old fears that prevented her from achieving a beautiful level of rapport with all canines, Penelope answered with meaningful insights into the doggy mind that could be utilized pragmatically.

"If you're afraid of a dog, don't try to mask it. The dog is going to know, so ask it to help you.

"I've had experiences where I've been bitten by dogs. I'm not going to approach every dog. I'm going to listen to their thoughts carefully and ask what they want. Do they want to be touched or not? Are they going to attack me?

"Obviously people get attacked by dogs. It's part of our experience.

"If you're fearful, many dogs will look at *you* as dangerous. They will say, 'Wait a minute! You're hiding something! You are afraid of me—and that must mean there is something wrong with you.'

"Some dogs will try to help you when you respond to them in fear, but many others will regard your apprehension as a threat.

"So you should be honest with your fear and say, 'I don't like the fact that you are rushing up to the fence and barking at me. I acknowledge that you are guarding your area. Can we be friends?'

"If you are just honest with them, you'll stop them right in their tracks."

Penelope Smith has said that the cornerstone of her work and the positive results that she has experienced with animals over the years has been her connection with them as total beings. In her opinion, the acknowledgement of the essential spirituality of animals is what grants her the ability to understand them.

"Non-human animals are not some lower form of life, living with only automatic reactions or stimulus-response programming," she insists.

Of course, Penelope acknowledges that animals are *different* from humans and they do experience the world differently.

"They are also individuals, who combine their physical 'species nature' with their own unique mental and spiritual qualities and awareness to express themselves and fulfill their purposes in this universe."

In her thought-provoking book, *Animals . . . Our Return to Wholeness,* Penelope readily concedes that it is a good thing to study the biological aspects of animals, but we must learn to see the whole being when we approach an individual of any species.

"When you make the spiritual connection," she says, "it's almost as if bodies disappear. They can be seen for what they are—vehicles for life in the physical and individual expressions of divine creation. When the essential, spiritual contact is made—being to being—a recognition of likeness, even oneness, occurs."

When one is able to develop an affinity with his animal friend and to nourish a deep respect, Penelope promises that something magical will happen which will engender open communication, trust, and understanding.

This type of relationship with our pets cannot come about if we treat them as babies or dependent underlings. We must learn to blend compassion and kinship.

"If you have experienced this kind of soulful communion with another creature of any kind, including human," Penelope states firmly, "you are, by your approach or attitude, acknowledging your union or your commonality as spiritual beings. Even if you don't know about it or phrase it in these terms, the animals know."

Of course even an experience of soulful communion or an attitude of compassion cannot guarantee that every animal you meet is going to blend with you or even wish to communicate with you. As we humans do, so do animals make their own choices, and "they have their conditioned fears from centuries of experience of their kind, plus their own personal experiences. . . . Some animals will be more aware of you as a spiritual being and have more ability to connect with you. Others don't particularly want to—or see the need to—relate to humans or any other species."

In spite of such individual objections to interspecies communication on the part of certain animals, Penelope Smith's personal experiences have taught her that if you "remain quiet, attentive but unobtrusive, respectful and willing to make a connection, most animals will be interested—or at least will accept you as a part of their environment."

Penelope warns against regarding animals as humans in furred or feathered clothing.

"They are themselves—individuals with different senses, forms of thinking, means of expressing themselves, and ways of seeing life. The joy comes when you connect spiritually and share each other's worlds. . . . You celebrate the experience of differences and rejoice in the oneness of your essential nature. This opens the door for learning from one another, sharing wisdom, and growing together in harmony."

SIX

Remarkable Reb, Beagle Extraordinary

Reb came to us from the busy streets of Chicago. The charming beagle fellow, apparently a homeless vagabond, had followed the younger son of an actress friend of ours home from the neighborhood grocery store. Since the dog was collarless, tracing any possible owner was impossible. Posters declaring a lost dog found proved to be unproductive.

Although our actress friend adored the dog as much as both of her sons did, she could endure no more than two weeks of the energetic four-legged guest in their crowded apartment.

Though she was beset with entreaties to keep the congenial guy, she was in the process of surviving an unpleasant divorce, and adjusting her once comfortable lifestyle from large house to medium-sized apartment was proving to be difficult enough with adding any bounding, bouncy four-legged complications. Besides, she already had what had always seemed to me to be one of the largest cats in the western world; and the prospect of adding a dog to living quarters already severely compressed was not nearly as positive as it might have been under other, more roomy circumstances.

Our friend decided that their uninvited beagle roommate needed the marvelous, unlimited outdoor expanses of Iowa in which to romp unrestrained, along with the company of our four children.

Although I was somewhat reluctant to acquire another dog at

that particular time due to the unfortunate circumstances under which we had recently lost Mitch, a mixed-breed shepherd, I yielded to her lavish descriptions of the high intelligence and congeniality of Rebel (since she was a bona fide southern belle, boasting the bloodlines of three Confederate generals in her family tree, she had already provided the beagle with a name she had deemed appropriate). Then, too, she told me that her older son was already packing the car for the long drive to northeastern Iowa to deliver him to our doorstep, hearth, and home.

I truly had second thoughts while we awaited the delivery of Rebel, Son of the Chicago Streets.

If he were a runaway or a maverick dog, why should I bring him into the midst of a family of four children, ages ranging from five to thirteen?

And what about the primary rule that every dog owner must follow without exception? *Always acquire a dog as a very young puppy.*

From the description provided over the telephone by our actress friend, Rebel was at least a year old.

She had not taken him to a veterinarian. Perhaps he bore all kinds of diseases that he had picked up on Chicago's mean streets.

If he had been trained by a previous owner and become lost or a runaway, then Rebel had already acquired a set of personal traits and idiosyncrasies that might not blend with our own. If he had always been a stray left to his own devices, then it might be exceedingly difficult to attempt to teach him anything.

By the time Rebel had arrived, I had drawn up a list of potential families on which I might foist him.

But he came walking into our front room with the tail-wagging ease of a natural charmer. His alert, merry eyes seemed to be saying, "Hello, I like you people already. I really hope you like me, because I believe we were made for each other."

I think all of us sensed at once that we were in the presence of an extraordinary personality. It was as if each of us could achieve almost instant rapport on a mental level. And each of the kids—thirteen-year-old Bryan, eleven-year-old Steven, nine-year-old Kari, and five-year-old Julie—experienced love at first sight.

I found myself speaking to him as if he were a newly arrived house guest and I was explaining where to find the clean towels.

"You may enter the kitchen, because the floor has indoor-outdoor carpeting. Your bowls for food and water will be in the porch just off the kitchen. Please do not enter the living room because of the new carpeting that will pick up your loose hair. You may have access to the upstairs, and your bed is in the large basket on the second-floor landing. We go to bed as late as possible and sleep as late as possible, so please, no early morning demands."

It was that simple. It was as if Rebel nodded complete and unprotested comprehension after each directive—and that was that.

And he never seemed to have minded that we almost immediately shortened his name to "Reb."

I was astonished to see the beagle listed as number 72 (out of 79) in order of intelligence in Stanley Coren's *The Intelligence of Dogs* (Free Press, 1994). There is no need to dispute the personal observations of Coren, a professor of psychology and a dog trainer, but it is at this point that I wish to make a few statements of my own regarding canine intelligence.

I have long believed that the intelligence of a dog is largely dependent upon the mental-spiritual linkup which occurs between the dog and its owner.

I am certain that we have all known dogs whom we suspected were innately more intelligent than their owners. And surely we all know that it is largely impossible to rank all members of any single breed as more intelligent than all other members of another breed. We have all seen what happens whenever some otherwise able professors and scholars attempt such distinctions of intelligence among human ethnic groups.

What I am suggesting is that the intelligence displayed by your dog will be directly proportional to the level of bonding which you have permitted between you and your canine companion. If you regard your dog as little more than an animated stuffed toy, then that is the level of intelligence that you will receive from him or her. If you consider your dog to be a bit more than a stuffed toy, perhaps something along the lines of an affectionate appliance, somewhat like a loving toaster or television set, then you are likely to receive an appropriate utilitarian response from Fido or Fifi.

But if you have found yourself a responsive dog (and, of course, there are degrees of sensitivity and responsiveness among canines just as there are among humans) and if you are willing to commit to an attitude of openness, a full expression of respect, a wish to be caring, and a willingness to give and to receive unconditional love, then you will witness a manifestation of intelligence from your canine beyond what you ever expected was possible. A beautiful, perhaps limitless, mind-link will occur which will allow you to gain a fuller understanding of the mysteries of God's continuing acts of creation.

I remember the time when an editor friend from New York was visiting us during the week of the Nordic Fest celebration in our little Iowa community. People were dressed in authentic Scandinavian costumes for the occasion, regardless of whether they were of Nordic, Irish, German, English, or African descent; and the town was filled with displays and booths honoring the old Viking traditions, paying tribute to the pioneer spirit, and offering tempting dishes of a large variety of ethnic food.

The children and their mother (Marilyn, who died in 1982) had already left to participate as marchers in the big Nordic Fest parade, and my friend and I trailed a bit behind, busily engaged in conversation.

We had walked a block or so from our house when I became aware of Reb following quietly behind us.

"Oh, Reb," I said in a quiet, apologetic voice. "I am so sorry, but you cannot come along on this walk. We are going to a place where there will be crowds of people. You would not really enjoy such hubbub, anyway. Please go back to the front steps and wait for us there. We won't be long."

Reb listened to my explanation, then, apparently satisfied with its truthfulness and sincerity, turned and walked back to the front steps to await our return with as much patience as possible.

My editor's eyes were wide with amazement. "That was incredible. You spoke to your dog just as you do your children. And he obeyed just as well. You didn't gesture. You didn't point. You didn't raise your voice. It was as if he understood every word that you spoke to him."

"Why not?" I teased. "Reb was born in this country, too."

Reb had an uncanny ability to perceive who among complete strangers to him were known or unknown to the family.

An unusually alert watchdog, Reb was on the case any time of the day or night. Although he barked only when it was absolutely necessary to sound an alarm, nothing seemed to get by his tireless scrutiny of our premises. Unsolicited visitors or salespersons arriving on our property would be unable to leave their vehicles unless one of our family authorized Reb to give permission to do so.

And yet Reb seemed to know if the occupant of the strange automobile was an old high school classmate I had not seen for fifteen years or a relative I had not seen since a family reunion twenty years before.

Somehow aware of my prior relationship with that person, he would approach the vehicle without barking or growling his usual warning. Instead, he would wag his tail in a friendly manner and cheerily usher the visitor to our front door.

Time after time, I witnessed Reb recognizing men and

women that he could only have perceived from my memory banks. While the skeptics will quickly argue that I perhaps provided visual clues of acceptance when the visitors arrived, I will stress the fact that I was always *inside* the house, most often working at my typewriter, while Reb was *outside,* alone with our unexpected guests. How our remarkable beagle could somehow ascertain at a glance which of the strangers were friends or relatives and which ones were uninvited salespeople will remain a mystery to our present methods of scientific analysis.

SEVEN

The Caretakers

In 1978, Susan Duncan of Bellevue, Washington, was stricken with multiple sclerosis.

Determined to lead as normal a life as possible, she became a health education teacher, married, and had two children.

But the nerve disorder continued to worsen. By the time she was in her mid-thirties, Susan frequently required a wheelchair. Most often she would walk with a cane, but she would fall down often—as many as fifteen times a day.

Then, in 1992, when she was visiting the local Humane Society shelter, she spotted a three-year-old stray German shepherd-Great Dane mix that she was informed was just days away from being put to sleep.

She found herself drawn to the huge dog—well over one hundred pounds—sitting in a cage. He seemed to be looking her right in the eye.

She entered the cage, and the giant mutt jumped up and plopped his massive paws down on her shoulders. Susan, who stands only five feet tall, was nearly knocked over.

Somehow, though, she knew that the colossal canine was not being aggressive. It was just his wacky way of being friendly.

Susan decided to adopt the congenial behemoth. She christened him Joey, and she hoped that she might be able to teach him a few simple tasks, such as carrying her books in a backpack and opening doors for her.

Joey mastered those chores in no time at all, and soon he was helping her get up in the mornings by clasping her pajama legs gently in his mouth and pulling her feet to the edge of the bed. He was also able to open dresser drawers and to fetch requested items of wearing apparel. And it wasn't long before Joey was answering the telephone and helping Susan shop in the grocery store.

And most important of all, Joey was always there with his great strength to help Susan to her feet when she fell down.

Linda Hines, executive director of the Delta Society, a national organization dedicated to promoting awareness of the ways in which animals help humans, said that their group named Joey the Assist Dog for 1994. "Susan saved Joey's life," Ms. Hines told journalist Don Gentile. "Now he's saving hers."

Sheep Dog Brings Rachel Back from a Five-Week Coma

It was every parent's worst nightmare.

On Labor Day 1992, John and Sheila Morrison decided to treat their pretty eleven-year-old daughter Rachel to a roller coaster ride at an amusement park in Grand Prairie, Texas. And then, as the car in which they were riding whipped around a bend, Rachel was thrown out. In horror they watched helplessly as she plummeted to the ground twenty-five feet below.

The doctors were not optimistic, and their words were far from encouraging. The Morrisons were informed that their daughter had suffered severe brain damage.

The tragic bottom line was that she might not live. And if she did, the medical experts warned, she might be a vegetable for the rest of her life.

On October 7, Rachel began undergoing pet therapy at the Baylor Institute for Rehabilitation in Dallas. The director of the program, Shari Bernard, brought a number of dogs to the comatose girl, and Rachel slowly began responding to a few simple commands.

Although striving to remain positive, it was sadly apparent

that the child's responses were scarcely more than robotlike and that she still gave little evidence that she was in touch with her environment. Most often, Rachel would simply sit still in her wheelchair, mute and unresponsive.

Then, on October 14, Shari brought Belle, a lively Australian sheepdog, to Rachel's side.

Shari told reporter Philip Smith how the girl had slowly reached out to put her arm over Belle.

"I said that Australian sheepdogs have no tails," Ms. Bernard said. "Then I asked Rachel what Belle was missing. And she suddenly whispered, 'A tail.'"

Shari Bernard could barely hear those first softly uttered words, but she was certain that she had heard Rachel break her long silence.

She admitted that she was stunned. It was as if Belle had somehow been able to penetrate the deep recesses of the child's consciousness and enable her to speak again. Rachel's first words since Labor Day came out very slowly, as if forced from deep within her.

That evening, to the unrestrained joy of Sheila Morrison, she was able to speak to her daughter on the telephone.

Shari Bernard told reporter Smith that in the eight years that she had worked in pet therapy at the Baylor Institute for Rehabilitation, she had never witnessed a case quite so dramatic as that of Rachel's: "It was as if there was a special bond between them."

Rachel, who continued to make steady progress, said simply, "I love being with dogs. Belle made me want to speak again."

Trixie Kept Her Paralyzed Master Alive for Nine Days

Jack Fyfe, a seventy-five-year-old resident of Sydney, Australia, lay dying of thirst after a massive stroke. If it had not been for Trixie, his six-year-old Australian Kelpie–Border collie mix, who brought him water, he would surely have died.

Jack's living nightmare began when he awakened to find the left side of his body completely dead. He felt as if the roof had caved in on him and crushed him to his bed, and he realized that he must have had a stroke while he was sleeping.

He tried to roll out of bed, hoping that he might be able to drag himself to the telephone, but he was totally unable to move.

That was when the horror of his predicament truly struck him. He lived alone and was not expecting any visitors. He was invited to a social event at his daughter's, but that was nine days away. He was unlikely to be missed for those nine days!

Jack became frantic. His screams for help were barely more than ineffective whispers.

It was so very hot in the house, probably over ninety degrees. He was likely to die an agonizing death of thirst long before anyone missed him.

After a few hours, he pitifully cried out for water while he drifted in and out of consciousness.

And then a most remarkable thing occurred.

Trixie, who had hovered near Jack's bed, whining in helpless canine sympathy, suddenly left the room. Jack could hear her slurping water from her bowl in the kitchen. And then in a few moments she returned, jumped upon Jack's bed, and released a snoutful of water into his mouth.

Jack recalled that the sensation of the water reaching his parched lips and throat was wonderful. He had often repeated the word *water* as he filled Trixie's bowl, but for her to interpret his gasping of the word as a request for her to fetch water seemed a miracle.

For days, each time Jack called out for water, Trixie heeded his request. When the water bowl ran out, the resourceful dog got a towel and dipped it in the toilet bowl.

Jack was not particular about the source of the life-preserving liquid. He thankfully sucked on the soaked towel as if he were a helpless baby.

On the ninth day after his debilitating stroke, Jack Fyfe heard Trixie barking at people at the front door. His daughter had missed him and brought paramedics along with her. He was saved.

Jack's attending physician and his daughter saw that there was no question that the senior citizen had been kept alive solely through the attentive ministrations of his faithful dog. And Jack himself rested more comfortably knowing that his indomitable Trixie would always be there for him.

Dogsled Team Hauls Cyndi Around Snow-Swept Alaska in a Wheelchair

Although thirty-one-year-old Cyndi Irish of North Pole, Alaska, has been paralyzed from the waist down since 1982, she confidently declares that she is not "a fixed object." When the snow covers the streets and roads in the north country where she resides, she simply hitches up her black German shepherd Max and her mixed-breed brindle-colored husky Girl Dawg to her wheelchair, shouts a cheery, "Mush, you huskies!" and away they go.

Determined not to permit her disability to deny her from enjoying the beauty of the countryside around North Pole, about two hundred sixty miles north of Anchorage, Cyndi attaches miniature chains to her chair's wheels for traction, and puts her dogs into harness.

Cyndi told reporter John Blackburn that she had always been an active person, and her marvelous canine caretakers, Max and Girl Dawg, allow her to receive a different but "exhilarating" version of a brisk walk.

Karen Piper, who was responsible for training Girl Dawg to pull the wheelchair, said that the dogs helped Cyndi to preserve a sense of independence and the knowledge that she did not have to rely on anyone else to help her get around.

German Shepherd Saves Baby's Life Twice in Nine Months

Peter is such an attentive caretaker that he saved tiny Tiffany Burns's life twice—just nine months apart.

Infant Tiffany was only nine days old when the young German shepherd came running into her mother's bedroom and got her to follow him back to the child's crib.

Joan Burns of Sioux Falls, South Dakota, was horrified to find her baby blue in the face and lying very, very still. Thanks to Peter, she got to the crib in time to perform CPR on her infant daughter and to save her life.

Concerned about the infant's overall health, Joan had earlier had her doctor carefully examine Tiffany. Although nothing was discovered that indicated any serious abnormality or medical condition, Peter had seemed ill at ease and insisted on sleeping under Tiffany's crib.

Looking back on the frightening experiences, Joan Burns said that it was as if Peter had known that little Tiffany required special attention.

Such a demand for special attention arose again one night about nine months later. Once again Peter came bounding urgently into the master bedroom to awaken the sleeping mother.

Joan gave Tiffany a cursory once-over and decided that everything was fine.

But when she tried to return to bed, Peter blocked her path. How unlike the German shepherd to be so aggressive and demanding.

The puzzled mother spent more time, carefully examining her daughter. Nothing. Tiffany was fine.

But Peter, in German shepherd body language, said no way.

Joan pushed past him, wanting very much to return to bed and sleep.

Peter kept at her until she got up once again, this time quite irritated, to go into Tiffany's bedroom to conduct a third examination of the sleeping infant.

"And it was during my third time checking Tiffany that I was horrified to discover that my baby had stopped breathing—just like the time nine months before! I performed CPR with Peter assisting me by licking Tiffany's face.

"Later, the doctors theorized that Peter's licking helped stimulate her to breathe again."

This time, after the doctors completed their examination of little Tiffany, their diagnosis discovered symptoms of a rare infant sleeping disorder.

Since the narrow escape of the second episode, Tiffany sleeps with a special monitor that emits a beeping sound if she should cease breathing.

Peter, however, magnificent canine caretaker that he is, is taking no chances. He still sleeps under Tiffany's crib.

Trapped and Helpless in a Ravine: Her Dog Honey Shared Her Ordeal

Although Linda Myers suffers from muscular dystrophy and is confined to a wheelchair, the drive on September 12, 1991 from New Britain to Amston, Connecticut, held no special challenges or threats for her. The van was equipped with a CB radio and a car phone if anything should go wrong; and besides, she had brought her dog Honey along to keep her company.

She had enjoyed visiting friends, but it had gotten late. At 2:00 A.M., she called her fiancé Donald on the car phone to let him know that she was on her way home.

Linda had traveled only about a mile, however, when she was startled to see a tractor-trailer's headlights glaring in her back window. The careless truck driver pulled ahead, moved to the middle lane, then thoughtlessly swerved back in front of her.

Seeking desperately to avoid a crash, Linda veered to the right and lost control of the van.

She remembered skidding off the road and smashing through

a guardrail. In a sickening moment of horror, she felt the van crash on its side.

The impact of the fall threw her against the windshield—and then everything went black.

When Linda regained consciousness, she found that she was lying on the passenger side. The lights were on, and she could see by her watch that she had been out for about twenty minutes.

Although it felt as though some fiend had bludgeoned her several times with a baseball bat, Linda was able to assess her physical situation and determine that she had not suffered any critical injuries. Realistically, though, she knew that she was too battered and too weak to attempt to climb up to the road.

Honey was there, snuggling up against her. She would stay with her.

Thank God, they had both survived the accident.

Later, Linda would learn that the van had plunged down a 438-foot embankment, rolling over ten times before crashing to a stop.

She tried calling Don on her cellular phone. He would be able to bring help.

But she was too far down in the ravine for her cellular phone to transmit properly.

She managed to reach her CB, but its battery went dead before she could rouse anyone to come to their aid.

Linda did her best to keep negative thoughts from her mind. Although she was very frightened, she kept telling herself that she and Honey would be found before terribly long.

She knew that it was going to be a cool Connecticut September night. She had heard a weather forecaster predict that the temperatures would drop down into the forties.

Honey cuddled up against her to help keep her warm. With teeth chattering in the chill night, Linda sang hymns at the top of her voice to help stay calm and to keep her spirits high.

"If it wasn't for Honey, I probably would have given up hope," Linda said later. "She cuddled up against me and kept me warm. Every once in a while, she'd lick my hands as if to say, 'Don't worry. I'm here.' "

The next morning, along with some nice, warm sunshine, an idea popped into Linda's head, as if God had heard her pleas and told her what to do: she hooked up her CB radio to the battery in her wheelchair.

It worked!

And after Linda had repeated her call for help over and over, a truck driver heard her desperate message and crawled down the ravine to rescue her.

Doctors later discovered that Linda had sustained a broken rib during the crash. She was thankful that she was alive and that she and the faithful Honey had survived a twelve-hour ordeal at the bottom of a steep ravine.

Pearl the Poodle Nursed Kimberly Through a Serious Illness

Kimberly Marooney of San Diego, California, wrote to inform me that when she got Pearl, a four-pound white poodle, she was in the middle of a long illness and home alone every day.

"She became my companion, my protector," Kimberly said, "and she taught me much about her gift of unconditional love. At my hardest and most painful moments, Pearl would perch on my stomach, barking, as if she could bark away my suffering. When I cried, she would lick my tears away as she tried to comfort me. She spent many long hours curled up next to me, as if to say with her very presence, 'I am here for you.' "

Kimberly stated that Pearl is so perfect physically that the only thing saving her from a life of dog shows and breeding is her small size.

"She's about two pounds too small in her judging class, and the dog breeder who had previously owned her recognized that she did not have the right personality for a kennel dog.

"How true that has proven, for she is truly an angel in dog disguise. Pearl shares her gift of love so powerfully that it is hard to believe that it comes from such a small being."

Kimberly confessed that she enjoys taking Pearl out in public because the little poodle attracts people from every possible background.

"They all come up and bask in her love, and I watch their expressions shift from that of the pain in their lives to that of joy. Hardness softens as smiles light up. Then they tell me a story about a poodle that belonged to their grandma or mom. By the end of the conversation, I feel as if I have a new friend."

Now that Kimberly has recovered from her long and painful illness, she has a new career in writing. Though she is still home alone all day, Pearl continues to be her ever-present companion.

"Whether I am doing research or working on the computer, Pearl is curled up next to me. She also reminds me when it is time to take a break for a few minutes of loving play."

Kimberly Marooney's favorite times together with Pearl are those moments designated for meditation.

"She notices the shift in my vibration when I meditate, and she wants to be right in the center, in my lap or often on my chest. She gazes into my eyes with a perfect sense of knowing as we share the divine energy. I feel so blessed to have her in my life. She is truly an angel of love."

EIGHT

Medical Science Agrees: Dogs Are Good for Your Health!

In her *Notes on Nursing* published in 1860, Florence Nightingale, the British reformer of hospital nursing, advised her readers that a dog provided an excellent companion for the sick.

We dog lovers do not need to rely upon anecdotal evidence to support our belief that a loving relationship with a dog is good for our bodies and our souls. For over one hundred years, serious representatives of orthodox medical science, such as the famous Ms. Nightingale, have been agreeing with us that dogs are good for our health.

A recent three-year study that set out to *disprove* claims that dog owners were healthier than folks lacking canine companions ended up agreeing that claims of the curative powers of dogs were both accurate and valid.

At an international medical conference held in Montreal in the summer of 1992, Dr. Warwick Anderson of Australia's Baker Research Institute announced findings which demonstrated that male owners of dogs had significantly lower levels of blood triglyceride, cholesterol, and systolic blood pressure.

Dr. Anderson stated that the gentle action of petting one's dog can assist in reducing blood pressure and heart rate. The simple and natural act of petting your pooch also stimulates a soothing sensation of well-being—a response of ancient origin that is believed to have been derived from the relaxing ambiance achieved during the process of mutual grooming that our human ancestors performed on one another.

In his analysis of more than five thousand patients, Dr. Anderson found that dog owners had "significantly reduced levels of known risk factors for cardiovascular disease."

Veterinarians have known for years that a dog's heart rate and blood pressure drop dramatically when it is stroked or petted, so the scientific proof that contact with our dogs can do the same for us is wonderful news. Such research proves that being friendly with Fido eases stress, changes body chemistry, and cuts the risk of cardiovascular disease.

Dogs Reduce Stress in Women Even Better Than Their Best Friends Can

Although there may be certain therapeutic benefits to ladies getting together to commiserate on the complexities of life over a cozy cup of coffee, Dr. Karen Allen, associate professor in the School of Medicine at the State University of New York at Buffalo, recently announced her findings that a dog can help women put a leash on stress far more effectively.

In a series of revealing tests, forty-five women had their blood pressure, pulse, skin response, and other body functions monitored while they worked on a number of brain-teasing arithmetic problems designed to produce stress and tension. Some of the women tackled the problems with just their dog with them in the testing room. Others performed the tasks in the company of a human friend. Interestingly, body responses remained normal among those women who worked with only their dogs present. But women who had a human friend present showed dramatically increased physiological response. Even the presence of a very close, supportive human friend caused increased blood pressure, pulse rate, and palm-sweating in these stressful problem-solving situations.

Why was this so?

Dr. Allen pointed out that we know very well that our dogs don't judge us or evaluate us, and they certainly couldn't care less how we might do on an arithmetic test.

Even though the friends of the women subjects sat next to them, made no comments, and offered support through eye contact and posture, the women being tested still demonstrated an increase in blood pressure, pulse rate, and other physical expressions of stress. The very presence of these friends made the subjects more likely to rush through the problems and make mistakes.

Dr. Allen said the results clearly demonstrated that the ease with which the tasks were accomplished was much more pronounced with a dog present.

Dogs make us laugh and help us not to take life too seriously—things that definitely aid us in times of stress and tension.

"Of course, it's still important to be able to turn to a good friend for support, comfort, and advice," Dr. Allen told journalist Larry Masidlover, "but I can think of many special situations where I would rather be with my dog."

Getting a Dog Can Save Your Marriage

In a study somewhat similar to Dr. Karen Allen's, University of Pennsylvania researchers determined that stressed-out couples who were attempting to salvage their troubled marriages were less tense and angry when a dog was in the room. They were also much more successful in discussing their marital differences than those couples who tried negotiating without a dog present.

Dr. Alfred Coodley, a clinical professor emeritus of psychiatry at the University of Southern California School of Medicine, told journalist Peter Fenton that having a dog can improve marriages whether the couples are unhappy or very much in love. "Just petting a dog significantly lowers blood pressure, heart rate, and muscular tension," Dr. Coodley said. "These physical changes make you feel calmer, able to handle problems in your marriage better. This means improved communication, which helps you and your mate talk more openly with far less disagreement."

Having a dog around the house can display your more endearing qualities and thus make you seem more appealing to your spouse. A dog is not critical or judgmental, so it is much easier to relax, to become more playful, and to show affection. Such loving qualities may then be transferred more readily to your spouse.

Dogs Can Accurately Predict the Onset of Epileptic Seizures

In September 1991, at the annual congress of the British Veterinary Association held in Torquay, Devon, one of the world's leading veterinarians reported that there were many documented cases on record of dogs accurately predicting an oncoming epileptic seizure in their owners—even before their owners themselves detected the first indications of an episode. Andrew Edney, president of the World Association of Small Animal Veterinary Organizations, stated that dogs were so successful in detecting oncoming seizures that there was enormous potential in establishing studies to identify future "predictor" dogs for use as companions for epileptics.

Elizabeth Rudy, a veterinarian from Seattle, who is herself an epileptic, is made aware of an oncoming seizure by her golden retriever Ribbon. If they are indoors and Ribbon senses that Elizabeth is about to have a seizure, he will come to her, lick her hands, and stare at her. If they happen to be outdoors, Ribbon will stop walking and put his ears down.

The executive director of the Epilepsy Institute in New York, Reina Berner, told of a patient who at one time was afraid to leave her home and venture outside because her seizures caused her to fall. But then her dog appeared to develop an ability to sense the imminent attack, and he would begin barking frantically until his owner sat down. Now the patient is able to leave her home, secure in the knowledge that her dog will be certain to warn her of an impending seizure in time to ready herself before its onset.

No Special Training Is Necessary: Somehow Dogs "Know"

In the spring of 1993, the Veterinary Record published the results of a survey of thirty-seven dog owners conducted by Andrew Edney in which he determined that although *none* of their dogs had been formally trained to respond to their owner's seizures, twenty-one of them often appeared apprehensive or restless prior to the onset of such a seizure, and twenty-five made dramatic attempts to attract attention for their owners once a seizure had begun.

Scientific speculation about how untrained dogs could so accurately predict the onset of epileptic seizures in their owners includes the possibility that observant and sensitive canine companions can sense the bioelectrical disturbances experienced by humans undergoing an epileptic episode.

Other researchers have suggested that epileptics may emit a characteristic odor prior to a seizure. Although this odor may be undetectable to other humans, it is noticed by the more sensitive nose of their dogs.

Canines May Also Sense the Subtle Signs of Hypoglycemic Coma

Many insulin-injecting diabetics affirm that their dogs can detect sharp falls in their blood sugar in sufficient time for them to ingest carbohydrates and thus prevent them from slipping into a hypoglycemic coma. Once again, some theorists have suggested that an olfactory trigger is responsible.

In those cases involving detection of their owner's approaching hypoglycemia by dogs that were being held in their master's or mistress' arms, it is possible that the animals have reacted to sudden changes in body temperature experienced by their owners.

Dogs Not Only Offer Cheer in Cancer Wards, They May Also Be Able to Detect the Dread Disease

Hospices for the terminally ill have recently begun relying on four-legged therapists in steadily growing numbers. Dogs bring back humor and life to those whose existence has been dulled by pain.

Pam Currier, a former hospice director, commented on a dog that they had regularly brought in for their patients: "For the lonely patient, she was a friend. For the depressed patient, she was a clown. For the anxious patient, she was a diversion. Patients who had been undergoing treatment for many months found in her someone to cherish."

Rose Griffith, nursing director of the Hospice of St. John in Lakewood, Colorado, told journalist Glenn Troelstrup that some of the most impressive emotional healing that she had ever witnessed had been brought about by a dog named Inky, a ten-pound Chihuahua mix. Since she was trained for the task in mid-1986, Inky has made three daily healing rounds at the fifty-bed hospice. Human staff members say that their canine colleague has an uncanny sense of who needs her the most and precisely what her bedside response should be.

Hospice spokesman Peter Wellish commented that it was truly a great tragedy how many patients die without loved ones by their side. For such terminally ill men and women, a canine therapist is a true blessing.

"Dying patients don't seem to demand much. All the riches

and money in the world are no longer important. Quality time is what matters most. For those patients who really need her, Inky will spend the entire night. If there are two who need her, she will intuitively divide her time between them."

The idea of incorporating the services of a canine therapist to help the dying at the Hospice of St. John first belonged to Sister Helen Reynolds of the Sisters of Loretto. She found the beloved Inky in a humane society shelter where she would soon have been put to death.

Sister Helen knew that she wanted a dog "who wouldn't hesitate to jump into people's laps, who would spread love instinctively and impartially . . . We'll never know how many patients died easier, how many grieving families were counseled more, how many nurses were strengthened to carry on—all because of a bundle of love named Inky."

Dr. Leo Bustad of the College of Veterinary Medicine at Washington State University has observed the amazing healing power of dogs: "The presence of a dog has a remarkable effect and seems to block pain. Dogs have been used in cancer wards with particularly impressive results."

Dr. Hywel Williams, a staff physician in the dermatology department at King's College Hospital in London, has theorized that melanomas might emit a particular odor that sensitive dogs might be able to "sniff out."

Among the recent cases that has given rise to Dr. Williams' provocative hypothesis is that of forty-seven-year-old Bonita Whitfield who was alerted to a serious skin cancer by Baby, her mixed-breed dog.

It seems that whenever Bonita was walking about in the privacy of her home in shorts or in her undies, Baby would start to whine and attempt to bite her on the thigh.

Baffled, because she knew Baby only as a gentle dog who had never before made a move to bite anyone, Bonita scolded her dozens of times before she noticed that Baby appeared to be after only a mole on her thigh. She had never really noticed it because it was toward the back of her thigh and out of her normal vision—but Baby seemed determined to nip the mole out of her flesh.

When Bonita Whitfield at last had the mole removed at King's College Hospital in London, she was informed that it was a malignant melanoma and the surgeons had removed it before it could spread. There was no question that Baby had saved her life by pestering her about the mole.

Fascinated by Ms. Whitfield's dramatic account of her dog's preternatural ability to detect a malignant melanoma, Dr. Hywel Williams announced his intention to initiate a study to investigate whether or not sensitive dogs could really detect skin cancer in their owners. If the study proves to be successful, there may be a place for dogs in a screening process for malignant melanomas.

Dogs Are Essential to Happiness for People Over Fifty

A nationwide survey of six hundred men and women over the age of fifty found dogs to be essential to happiness.

Fifty-seven percent of those surveyed by Carol Morgan of the Strategic Directions Group, a Minneapolis-based marketing firm, said that their dogs were very important to their quality of life.

Heart Patients Live Longer If They Own a Dog

Researchers at the University of Pennsylvania found that elderly heart patients live much longer if they have a dog to keep them company.

Bereavement Is Easier to Endure with a Dog

A report published in the Journal of Personality and Social Psychology revealed that bereaved patients who own a dog make far fewer visits to the doctor.

Dog Owners Visit Their Doctors 21% Less Often

In general, dog owners seek medical care an amazing 21 percent less often than people who live without canine companionship.

Your Dog Is Your Four-Legged Medicine Kit

Experts writing in the University of Texas Lifetime Health Letter conclude that spending time with your dog lowers your blood pressure, eases depression, and stimulates the production of endorphins, your body's natural tranquilizers. Even the casual stroking of your dog can produce immediate stress relief.

NINE

Eerie Footsteps on the Stairs for Queen, Reb, and Rascal

One night when I was thirteen, I was home alone with only Queen for company. We were living in Uncle Frosty's house at that time. He and Aunt Marie had moved in with Grandma Dina in the big house in town, and a hired man and his family were living in the old house on our home place.

I can't recall exactly why it was that I was alone that night, but I can remember enjoying myself by curling up in the big chair in my room with a copy of Frontier Stories and a bag of cinnamon balls.

Queen was seldom allowed in the house, and she was never allowed in the carpeted rooms or upstairs. On very cold winter nights, she was let in to sleep in the basement.

Knowing that my parents and sister would not be home for quite some time on this very cold winter's night, I confidently broke one of the strictest of family rules and allowed Queen to join me in my room on the second floor. I felt certain that no harm could be done by permitting Queen to enjoy a respite from basement decor. Besides, I knew that she just had to be lonely down there all alone.

I was deep into an exciting tale of a mountain man trying to escape pursuing Blackfoot warriors when I heard a peculiar noise that sounded very much like someone or something bumping into the kitchen table.

Queen heard it too. Her ears were pricked up straight, and she was moving her head quizzically from side to side.

All my other senses were on hold as my ears strained to hear any subsequent noises.

Then I heard the sound of a solid step on the stairs.

Someone was in the house and trying to creep up the stairs. And whoever it was quite obviously knew that I was upstairs all alone.

Nervous sweat broke out all over my body.

I knew that it wasn't my parents and sister coming home early. I had a clear view of the road from my room. I would have seen their headlights coming down the lane. Besides, they wouldn't creep quietly into the house and try to sneak up the stairs to bed. They would shout out that they had come home, and they would wish me goodnight.

Now, under more pleasant weather conditions, I might have suspected that a mischievous buddy or two might be playing a joke on me, planning on giving me a scare. But I was certain that none of my friends from neighboring farms would set out on a cold winter night across frozen, snow-packed fields and risk frostbite for the sole purpose of giving me a fright.

Whoever was in the house had to be an unwelcome intruder. A burglar. An axe-murderer. Who knew?

And whoever it was had just advanced two or three more steps!

That was enough for Queen. A snarling bundle of white rage, she ran from my room.

She ignored my shouts to stop, to stay in my room. She was set to do battle.

I expected her to charge down the stairs and rip into whomever might be there, but I could tell from the sound placement of her angry barking that she still remained at the top of the stairs.

I cautiously peered out of my room. Queen's hair was bristled; her teeth were bared.

But something was keeping her from charging our uninvited

guest. Something was holding her at the top of the stairs. Some instinctive sense of caution was urging her to stay put.

I had never seen anything intimidate Queen, but it certainly appeared as though something was giving her a reason to hold back and proceed with care.

The footsteps suddenly became louder, as if our invader were deliberately stamping his feet in an attempt to frighten Queen.

The loud noises only served to make Queen angrier and to growl and bark all the louder.

But the stamping sounds most certainly frightened me.

I didn't know what else to do other than to grab my .22 slide-action Winchester rifle. A face-to-face encounter with the intruder seemed inevitable. I prayed to God that I wouldn't have to use the rifle, but I had to consider very strongly the awful possibility that the invader might be armed. If that were so, I prayed earnestly that my being armed might result in a stand-off, and he would leave the house—and us—alone.

Judging by the sounds on the stairs, whoever had violated the sanctity of our home was standing just one step below the landing. A couple more steps and he would burst into view.

It seemed as though I could hear his labored breathing, perhaps even a grunt or two.

Queen's snarling increased in intensity, as if our unseen adversary had cursed at her.

My heart was pounding my chest so hard that it hurt. Although the temperature in the house was cool, I was dripping sweat. I felt for a moment or two as though I would faint.

And then I thought to look at the window directly behind the landing. I should have been able to see a reflection of our invader—but I saw nothing. There was no one on the stairs.

My senses swam dizzily. Both Queen and I had clearly heard footsteps ascending the old wooden steps leading upstairs. What was more, we could still hear hoarse, gasping breaths.

I don't know what got into me, but I suddenly shouted, "Charge!" and ran down the steps, my rifle at the ready. Barking the canine equivalent, Queen quickly passed me and ran ahead of me down the stairs.

I could hear the distinct sounds of footsteps beating a hasty retreat.

Queen was making the same kind of triumphant growling sounds that she made when she had a bull or a large boar on the run.

By the time that I reached the kitchen door, Queen was standing braced before it, barking a warning to *whatever* it was not even to think about coming back in the house.

In those untroubled times, farmers never thought about locking their doors. I instituted a change in our personal open-door policy when I slammed the bolt into place on the front door.

There would be no more reading of Frontier Stories that night. I sat in the kitchen, petting Queen, holding my rifle across my lap, until I heard the distinctive sounds of the family car coming down the lane.

I ushered Queen down to her basement dwelling before my transgression of family rules could be discovered, gave her a nice piece of supper roast as a reward for a security job well done, and positioned myself casually in front of the radio to await my parents and sister.

I had forgotten to unlock the door, however, and a great fuss was made and many playful accusations uttered that I must be afraid to stay home alone.

If only you knew! I thought to myself.

Although the invisible invader returned on two other occasions when Queen and I were home alone, I didn't tell my parents about the strange occurrences until many years later. On each subsequent visit, the ghostly visitor brought out the sweat on my forehead and accelerated my heart rate to the point where I felt as if I'd just run a four-minute mile.

Queen happened to be in the basement on both of the thing's return visits, and she went wild with rage at the sounds of the alien footsteps on the stairs once again threatening her young master.

On its third and final visit in that house, I sat waiting for it to climb the stairs to the very top step. Step by step, I listened to the invisible visitor come slowly up to the second-floor hallway.

I squinted my eyes, trying hard to make out some kind of image to go with the sound of the footsteps. Although I could see nothing, I suddenly shouted at full volume: "Get out of here! Get out and stay out!"

If the old legends are accurate when they state that creatures of the night cannot stay unless they are invited to do so, this entity knew that it was getting the bum's rush—and it departed quickly back down the stairs and out into the night.

I think I was in college when I finally told the family about Queen's and my encounters with the ghostly footsteps on the stairs. Interestingly, June confessed that Queen had also held the invisible whatever at bay at the door to her room on a couple occasions when she had been home alone.

Reb and Bryan Encounter Another Invisible Invader on the Stairs

Reb had been with us about four years when we moved to the farmhouse in the country outside of town. From the outside, the place was magnificent—a solid two-story home flanked by majestic pines that sat atop a grassy hill. At the foot of the hill was a picturesque creek with a small but sturdy bridge. Across the lane from the large barn was an old cabin that was said to be among the very first pioneer homes in the county.

But in spite of the house's trustworthy appearance and its inviting front porch, there was something about the place that made me feel uneasy. As soon as I entered the house, I felt that a death had occurred in a back room off the kitchen. The folks who sold us the house uneasily verified my impression.

I was concerned about the children, for I sensed that the psychic presence I detected, while certainly not evil, was not really a hospitable one either. If we were dealing with an earthbound spirit that resented new and different people moving into its home, then it might seek to work a little mischief on us.

Perhaps I should have become more concerned when, shortly before we were to move into the house, a cousin of the vacating family jokingly informed me that the home would be perfect for me.

When I asked exactly what he meant, he chuckled and asked rhetorically, "What better house could a writer of spooky books have than a haunted one?"

By this time, about 1973, I had already published numerous books on the paranormal and the unknown, and I had established an international reputation as a psychical researcher and chronicler of strange phenomena. While few of the townspeople would be able to understand the metaphysical thrust of my work, they could all comprehend that I wrote "spooky" books.

I was the first to undergo a visitation from the invisible forces of the psychic welcome wagon when I was alone at home one Sunday morning. What seemed to be violent explosions detonated throughout the big old house, from basement to attic and back again. They had me running around like crazy until I perceived exactly what was going on.

I was no longer the confused thirteen-year-old boy who stood trembling at the top of the stairs with his faithful dog Queen at his side. During my career as a psychical researcher, I had become quite well-versed in eerie but silly games that certain entities liked to play with humans, so I decided to do my best to ignore the noisy phenomena. Difficult as that proved to be, after about twenty minutes or so, the pseudo-explosions ceased and peace was restored to the farmhouse.

Three nights later, when I was working late at my office in town, I received an urgent telephone call from my older son, Bryan, who was home alone with Reb.

"Dad," he said, his voice warped by panic. "Reb and I are in my room. Someone has broken into the house and is coming up the stairs. I can hear him moving up the stairs, one step at a time."

Immediately I thought of my experience when I was thirteen and Queen and I faced down the mysterious invading footsteps coming up the stairs.

I also thought of my confrontation with the invisible pranksters just a few days before. It would appear that they were playing games again.

I could hear Reb's angry snarls in the background. Whatever was tormenting my son lay far enough beyond the bounds of the unseen world to be heard by our alert beagle guardian.

"Bry," I advised him, "try to stay calm. Whatever is coming up those stairs tried its game with me on Sunday. Your fear is feeding it. Distract your mind. Put on some music. Sing a song . . ."

"Dad," he interrupted my counsel, "I've got the shotgun. I'll shoot if whatever or whoever it is comes to the top of the stairs!"

My son's strained and frightened voice told me that I had better get out to the farmhouse as quickly as possible.

It had snowed earlier that day, and I prayed for no icy patches and no highway patrolmen. I was fortunate in both respects and managed to shave four minutes off the normal twelve-minute drive to the farmhouse.

The doors were locked from the inside, and Bryan was still barricaded in his room with Reb.

I yelled up from the back porch that it was I, and Bryan came down the stairs to unchain the back door.

I offered silent thanks that I had made it home before he had blown any holes in the walls—or himself.

Bryan still carried the 12-gauge shotgun, and he was visibly stressed by his ordeal. "Dad, something was in here. You know it wasn't my imagination. Reb heard it too. You could hear him growling at it and barking at it over the phone, right?"

After I had calmed him, I learned the full story of how Bryan and Reb had fallen victim to the invisible tricksters.

Bryan had been watching television when he heard what he assumed were the sounds of other family members returning home. With only partial attention, he listened to the familiar noises of an automobile approaching, car doors slamming, voices and laughter, and the stomping of feet on the front porch. Reb had sat up and was listening with cocked ears, whining softly in what Bryan assumed was anticipation of the family's return.

All of these sounds were so very natural, and the only thing that really caught at Bryan's attention and diverted it from the television program that he was watching was the peculiarity of the family approaching the front porch. He knew that of habit we all entered the house by the back and through the kitchen.

Then he was further surprised to hear loud knocking at the front door.

Everyone in the family had his or her own key, so why would anyone knock? And why would anyone be pounding at the front door when everyone usually entered through the back door?

When the knocking became more persistent, Bryan began to consider that it might not be the family at all. Perhaps some of his friends were driving in the country and decided to stop by unannounced.

Begrudgingly, Bryan stirred himself from his comfortable chair before the television set and went to admit whomever was at the front door.

He was astonished to find the front porch empty.

Just as he was about to step outside to investigate, he heard loud knocking at the back door.

Uttering a sigh of frustration, he slammed the front door and began to head for the kitchen and the back door.

He had taken no more than a few steps when the knocks were once again sounding at the front door.

By this time, Bryan began to assume that someone was playing a joke on him. He turned on the yard light so he could identify the jokesters' automobile.

He gasped when he saw that his was the only car in the driveway.

Fists were now thudding on both doors at the same time, and Reb was going wild, growling and baring his teeth at the bizarre intruders.

Bryan heard an eerie babble of voices and short bursts of laughter.

Whoever his tormentors were, they were now tapping on the windows as well as pounding on the doors.

And someone—or something—very large had opened the back door and was leaning heavily against the chain-lock, as if attempting to break it and force open the door.

That was when Bryan and Reb had barricaded themselves in his room and called me at my office.

After he had told me the details of his frightening ordeal, we walked around the outside of the house. We could easily determine that there were no footprints in the freshly fallen snow. There was no evidence of tire tracks other than mine in the lane, the driveway, or the yard.

No human agency had visited him, I explained, but rather some invisible, nonphysical intelligences that would initiate a spooky game with anyone who would play along with them.

Early the next evening, I gathered my four children and gave them instructions on how best to deal with any further ghostly mechanisms of sound or sight that might manifest themselves in the old farmhouse.

The basic strategy was to attempt to remain as indifferent and as aloof as possible to any eerie disturbances. In a positive but emphatic manner, one should indicate that he or she simply did not wish to play any silly games.

Under no circumstances should they become defiant or angry. The laws of polarity would only force the tricksters to come back with bigger and even more frightening demonstrations in response to the negative energy directed toward them.

Whether we were dealing with poltergeists, restless spirits in limbo, or an invasion of "nature spirits" mimicking human intelligence, I felt that I had given the kids sound advice in dealing with the unknown.

And although quite a repertoire of eerie events manifested for our individual benefits while we resided in that house, none of us was ever again caught completely off guard.

Alone in a 25-Foot Fire Tower with Her Dog— and a Ghost

Martha Dannell has told only a few close friends the complete story of the summer in the mid–1970s that she spent as a fire-spotter atop a twenty-five-foot tower in dense Oregon forest land. It was pretty rough living, and it got lonely, for her only companions were Rascal, her two-year-old Labrador—and a ghost.

"I lived atop that tower seven days a week for the entire summer," Martha said. "Since I graduated from college as a forestry technician, I wanted some really practical field experience as a fire-spotter. I was twenty-three that summer, so I thought the sooner the better."

Martha's living quarters were a fourteen-by-fourteen-foot cabin perched on top of the tower. She had no electricity and no running water, but she got by with a bed, a stove, a cupboard, a crank phone, and a transmitter radio.

"I had to pump my water from a fire pumper, so I recycled it about a half-dozen times. First I would heat it, then wash my hair. Next, I would take a bath, then use the water to wash out the cupboard and clean the floor."

Martha's watch covered a twelve-mile radius. If she spotted a fire, her job was to line up its location on the fire-finder and do her best to pin it down within forty acres. Then she called the ranger station so that someone there could notify the fire fighters.

* * *

She first heard the ghost late one night shortly after she had gone to bed.

"I had been there long enough to be able to identify all the normal, regular noises. What I heard sounded clearly like footsteps coming up the stairs to my cabin at the top of the tower. Rascal started to growl, so I know that he heard the sounds, too."

Martha got out of bed to investigate. "I knew there shouldn't be any rangers in the area that time of night, so whoever was coming up those stairs had absolutely no business doing so. Besides, the rangers would have called me first so they wouldn't scare me."

When she peered cautiously down the stairs, she saw no one.

"Rascal was still growling, but the stairs were empty. It took me quite a while to fall asleep that night, because I kept expecting to hear those footsteps again.

"But thank God, I had Rascal with me. He helped me keep my courage up."

The mysterious sound of footsteps became a regular feature of life in the forestry tower.

"I heard those sounds a lot, and so did Rascal. They actually became quite unnerving, and they kept me awake a lot of nights."

As it was, sleep was not all that easy to come by. Martha was also expected to provide weather and temperature checks as well as keeping a sharp eye out for fires.

"Every day, around two o'clock in the afternoon, I had to take the wind direction and speed, describe any cumulus clouds in the area, check the humidity, and indicate how much the temperature had risen or fallen. If there was a lightning storm, I might be up all night, checking for any hits that produced fires."

A lot of Martha's friends had asked her before she left for the forest tower if she wouldn't be afraid being out there alone in the woods all summer.

"About the only time I ever got scared was when I heard the ghost at nights. I never got used to the sounds of those footsteps coming up the stairs. And neither did Rascal. He would go nuts with growling at our invisible guest, and sometimes he would bark."

Once when she was on the crank phone with a ranger at the station, she admitted that she was hearing weird noises, like someone coming up the stairs.

"Oh no, not you too!" he said with a wry chuckle.

"What do you mean?" Martha asked. "Someone else has heard these sounds at night?"

"It's nothing," the ranger tried to dismiss her concern. "Seems like everyone who takes that tower has reported those same weird noises."

"So what causes them?"

"A ghost, I guess."

"That's not funny, ranger," Martha scolded him. "Do you want to come up here every night and babysit me?"

"Too hot this time of year," the ranger declined. "Last time I was up in that tower, it felt like it was over one hundred degrees."

"That's on a cool day," Martha agreed. "So tell me about the ghost. Were you serious?"

The ranger paused. "Oh, I don't know. Some of us guys have just called it the ghost of old Indian Joe."

"Who is—or *was*—he?"

"Well," the ranger continued, "there used to be an old Indian who lived alone by himself in that area. I don't know what his real name was, but he came to be like some kind of symbol of nature in the area. You know, like that Indian in those ads on television who cries when he sees what a mess us white guys have made of the environment.

"Anyway, this old fellow always used to be seen by everybody picking up trash and helping to keep things nice and natural-looking. One day someone noticed that we hadn't seen the elderly gent for a while, so we figured he must have died.

Since it wasn't long after that that the spotter who was in your tower started complaining about strange night noises, we told him that the ghost of the old Indian was just helping him do his job, looking out for forest fires and such."

The ranger's explanation of the eerie sounds was good enough for Martha.

"After that, Rascal and I would just call out to the noises and wish them a good night. Whatever—or *whoever*—was causing those spooky sounds, it made me feel a whole lot better to give some kind of benign identity to them. And doing so sure helped Rascal and me get through the long, hot summer in that tower."

TEN

Telepathically Locating a Missing Dog

Beverly Hale Watson of Charlotte, North Carolina, feels that her principal mission on Earth is to write spiritually inspired books and to teach others the wisdom of the mystery schools. As she continues to travel the road to enlightenment, the Lord blesses her with certain gifts for helping both humans and animals. From time to time, the Humane Society will contact her and request her special kind of help in locating a lost dog. That was how she came to know Luke, a beautiful Shetland collie.

"Luke, who was about seven years old, belonged to a family who had a small son," Beverly said. "The boy and the dog were inseparable. Luke slept with him, played ball with him, and he enjoyed accompanying father and son on automobile rides. Luke also had a real sweet tooth when it came to a chunk of cheese."

One Sunday afternoon, Luke and his human family traveled to visit grandparents in another city. Upon their arrival, everyone went into the house and quickly became engrossed in conversation, television programs, and other human activities.

"Unbeknownst to anyone," Beverly continued, "the back door had been left ajar. Luke decided that this was the perfect opportunity to go outside and roam around the backyard. Regretfully, the yard wasn't fenced, so Luke was free to wander. The problem was, the house was located in an area where all the homes looked the same from the back view.

"When he was tired of his roaming, Luke tried scratching on many neighbors' back doors, looking for his family, but to no avail. Numerous residents saw him wandering the neighborhood, but no one thought that the collie might be lost. Nor did anyone who opened their door to Luke's inquisitive scratching think to tie him up and try to find his owner."

As the story goes, Beverly said that quite a bit of time lapsed before Luke's owner realized that he was missing.

"An extensive six-hour search that afternoon and evening failed to locate the missing dog. It eventually came time when the family had to return home, not knowing what had happened to their beloved Luke."

Each day, the grandparents kept looking for the missing dog. In addition, articles on Luke were submitted to the local newspapers, and posters were tacked up in a wide variety of stores and on telephone poles and trees. Handbills were printed and distributed in mailboxes. Air time was obtained on radio. Many people said that they had seen a Shetland collie wandering around their neighborhood, but by the time they connected him to the missing Luke, the animal was gone.

After the family had suffered many days of distress over their lost dog, someone thought to call Beverly Hale Watson and ask her to utilize her very special talents.

"I met with the owner at a restaurant and designated on a map the area in which I sensed Luke to be traveling. From the moment that he told me about their missing collie, I was given a message that in due time he would be returned to his human family.

"Later, telepathically, I would pick up on what foods Luke was eating and where he was sleeping; but it took me some time before I was shown a specific location where he might be recovered.

"I could see psychically that Luke had found a pack of dogs to hang around with. It seems that he wanted to sow a few wild oats. He had set out on a bit of an adventure of exploration.

"Naturally Luke's family became most frustrated! I could describe Luke's health conditions and the places where he had been, but the days became weeks—and after nine weeks he was still missing.

"Although Luke and I had never met on the physical plane, I felt a strong attachment to him, and I kept receiving strong reassurances that he was all right, that he was fending for himself. I would pick up on locations where Luke was living, but when the owner went there, he was nowhere to be seen."

Quite unexpectedly, one day Beverly was given very specific visions of a place where Luke was being looked after by a group of neighbors who took turns feeding him.

"Actually, some kind people were seeing to it that Luke dined very well. I described the location in detail, giving prominent landmarks.

"As I continued to give the woman from the Humane Society the information that I was picking up telepathically from Luke, she said that she knew exactly the spot that I was describing.

"That evening, Luke's human family arrived on the scene and watched as their dear dog emerged from a wooded area. By this time all the kids in the neighborhood were eager to witness the reunion of Luke with his family, but unfortunately, because of the size of the crowd that had gathered, Luke became frightened and darted back into the woods."

Although Luke's owner tried very hard to coax him out of the woods and into his arms, he finally decided that it would be best if he returned the next evening at suppertime since that was the time when Luke would head for one of the local homes looking for food. He requested that no one in the neighborhood come outside at this time to distract the collie.

"The next evening, Luke's owner patiently waited for a couple of hours before the dog left the woods to seek his supper. He slowly got out of his car and started talking to Luke. The collie acted as though he recognized him, but he was still scared to come near him.

"After some more soft talk, the owner pulled a nice chunk of cheese out of a bag. The moment Luke saw his favorite treat, he ran up to his owner and the long-awaited reunion was accomplished."

The story of the family's successful efforts to locate their lost dog after two and one-half months made the front page of the local newspaper.

"I have no idea why I had such an unexplainable connection to this collie," Beverly admitted. "But it was a joyous day for me when he finally went home with his human family.

"Luke's owner called me to let me know that the collie couldn't wait to get in the car, and once he was home, he immediately greeted everyone. By the next day, Luke had fallen into his old routine as if nothing had happened."

Penelope Smith's avowed mission on Planet Earth is to help people return to their innate ability to communicate telepathically with other species.

While practically every dog owner speaks to his or her canine companion, Penelope Smith, pictured here with her friends Pasha and Rana, states that only a very few humans are willing to open their minds, lower the barriers of prejudiced thought, and listen to what their dogs may be saying to them.

Scott S. Smith, author of *Pet Souls,* with Scuffle, his terrier mix. Smith believes that as society evolves, we will increasingly "come to recognize animals as sovereign souls worthy of respect and peaceful coexistence . . . Interspecies communication, both scientific and psychic, will be the key to our coming down off our arrogant pedestal."

Since his earliest childhood, dogs have always been a part of author Brad Steiger's life.

Although farm life usually requires a larger dog, such as a collie or a shepherd, to help with the many chores, Brad's feisty little rat terrier Toby grew to prove equal to the robust challenges of herding livestock and driving off predators.

Queen was a wild dog who came to accept certain aspects of domesticated existence while demanding always to be treated with respect and as an equal. Once the "contract" was agreed upon, she never failed to pull her share of the work load and to guard the livestock with unfailing vigilance. Here she is as a pup, shortly after she accepted her "beautiful collar" as a sign of compliance to her human family.

As Brad trains his 4-H calf to be led by a halter, Queen keeps a sharp eye in case "Boris" decides to try to break away.

Reb, the remarkable beagle, loved to have his picture taken. As Brad's children posed for a Christmas card, Reb took advantage of a shutter's pause to include his presence as part of the holiday greeting. When Bonaparte the cat, who was equally a ham, saw the dog posing with the kids, he, too, decided to send his blessings for the holy season.

Author Sandra J. Radhoff is always troubled when she hears someone doubt that animals have spirits. She has included channeled messages in her book, *The Kyrian Letters,* that discuss the spiritual energies contained in the animal kingdom.

Beset with a host of physical maladies, the dignified Fred literally disappeared from the home of Patricia and Art Walton after sixteen years of intimacy with the family.

Although the seven wonderful years that Sandra spent with her German shepherd Sheila may have been only a brief moment in time, they taught her that love and the human heart are very expansive.

After suffering a period of mourning for their pet, Patricia and Art began to receive proof of Fred's survival after death. Among the manifestations of physical evidence were ghostly images of Fred that kept showing up in photographs.

Here in the reflection of clouds on a windshield, Patricia and Art see the image of their beloved Fred. If you look at the clouds in a twelve o'clock position, you can distinguish Fred's eyes, nose, mouth, ears, and so forth. "We know that he is waiting for us in Heaven," Patricia said.

From time to time, Beverly Hale Watson, the author of spiritually inspired books, is called upon by the Humane Society to use her special gifts to locate missing or lost pets. Although Luke, a Shetland collie, had been missing for nine weeks, Beverly's unique talents were able to reunite the dog with its humans.

Stormy the collie, Lori Jean and Charles Flory's angel in disguise.

Stormy, in the lead, heads down a rocky Colorado slope with Laddie in close pursuit.

Lori Jean and her husband Charles have seen the spirit image of their beloved Stormy on numerous occasions. Lori Jean says that collies come to teach love and to teach us to love one another.

Shortly after Beverly Hale Watson was forced to put her beloved black miniature poodle Toby to sleep, she received a message from him informing her when he would return in spirit. She is convinced that he has now come back to her in the form of another poodle named Joey.

One of Moses' favorite toys has always been a big red and white striped rubber "candy cane." Last summer when Brad and Sherry had to leave their black Lab in a local kennel while they traveled, Moses "loaned" his precious toy to a dog in a neighboring pen—who proceeded to chew it into tiny pieces. A new candy cane was first on Moses' Christmas list from Santa. Here, the Steigers' daughter, Melissa, helps Moses unwrap his prized present.

Moses became "King of the Road" when he helped Brad drive the moving truck from Cave Creek, Arizona, to Forest City, Iowa. For months afterward, it was difficult to make even the shortest of automobile trips without Moses begging to come along in the backseat.

Moses has never objected to one of Sherry's refreshing baths—especially in that 120-degree Arizona desert heat.

Brad and Moses are ready to run some errands. Brad has mail to drop in the post office; Moses has his rubber ducky to show everyone what a great retriever he is.

Janie Howard's sorrow over the loss of her beloved dog Rebel and the more recent death of her faithful Gratis (above) has been alleviated by her acquisition of Benediction, "Benny," for short.

ELEVEN

Learning to Communicate with Your Dog

The first time that I really noticed that our black Labrador Moses was an accomplished eavesdropper who probably understood nearly everything my wife Sherry and I said to him was one time in our backyard in Paradise Valley, Arizona, when I was playing catch with him.

One of my throws had gone wild and the rubber ball had landed in a low tree branch. Moses, misdirected by the throwing movement of my right arm, was running around looking in vain where he thought the ball must have landed.

I was feeling a bit mischievous, so I called out, "Where is it, Moses? Where is the ball? Go get it!"

As the trickster in me was having a quiet laugh at Moses' expense, Sherry came out of the house, quickly assessed the scene, and asked, "Where is the ball?"

Laughing out loud, but not raising my voice, I answered in a quiet voice, "It's in the tree by the wall."

Although he was several feet from me, Moses suddenly got an "aha" gleam in his eyes. He ran directly to the tree in question, spotted the ball, gave a powerful jump, and snatched it from the branch with his strong teeth.

Sherry and I were astonished. It appeared as though Moses had completely understood my answer to Sherry's question.

I hadn't gestured with my hands, pointed to the branch, or made any visual clue to the whereabouts of the ball; yet Moses, upon overhearing my disclosure of the ball's location, went directly to it and retrieved it.

And it must be mentioned that I hadn't specified in my response to Sherry in *which* tree and in which branch the ball rested. There were four large trees against the wall. The ball could conceivably have been in any one of them. Since I hadn't had time to inform Sherry which of the four trees held the coveted ball, somehow the words heard by Moses must also have carried with them the image of the precise tree and branch. Or, more likely, Moses understood *both* my spoken words and the image that my *mind* held of the ball in the branch.

As an aside, this seems an appropriate place to mention that I have never sought to train a dog to do tricks, to sit up, roll over, beg, and so forth. I have never even taught a dog to fetch, and I would not have been doing so with Moses except for the fact that as a retriever, he dearly loves to play catch and fetch.

But if I had thrown a ball for Queen or Reb, they would have looked at me with disdain, as if to ask, "If you wanted the ball, why did you throw it away? And now you want *me* to fetch it for you! Why? So you can just throw it again? Forget it. If you want the ball, *you* go fetch."

Now I am not at all smugly or arrogantly scolding those dog owners who derive satisfaction from training what I hope are their willing and cooperative dogs to perform acts deemed to be somehow representative of canine talent. But what has always mattered most to me has been the attainment of the highest possible level of quality communication between me and my four-legged brother or sister. And I am speaking of a quality of communication at least similar to that which I earnestly seek between myself and my human family and friends.

Although I very much appreciate honesty and loyalty from my human friends, I have never, to my immediate recollection, required any one of them to perform a balancing act, one-armed handstand, or anything of the sort to please me or to win my confidence.

Although I always expected truthfulness, respect, and courtesy from my human children, I cannot recall ever demanding that they beg for their meals to convince me that they were truly hungry. And they knew that the best way to convince me that they were deserving of their weekly allowances was not to roll over or fetch, but to demonstrate that their respective rooms were clean and their individual chores properly performed.

And so it has been with my canine children. I guess that I have always been a curious mixture of pragmatist and idealist. I think often of the wise words of my late friend, Sun Bear, the Chippewa Medicine Priest, who said, "If your Medicine [that is, magic] cannot grow corn, what good is it?"

While you have to be an idealist to believe in the power of Medicine in the first place, what good is it unless you can use it to earn your daily bread?

And why waste time and energy forcing your dog to amuse you with useless physical manuevers when the reason you wanted him or her in the first place was to bring a special kind of companionship, joy, and love into your life?

I want my dog to be there for me, and I will do my best to be there when it most needs me.

I have a firm agreement with Moses. I have promised not to ask him to walk up stairs on his front paws or to balance a ball on his nose to prove that he is truly a well-trained and obedient dog, and he has promised not to ask me to overhaul our car's engine or to rewire the electrical system in our house to prove that I am a real man.

* * *

It was while we were living in the rough and wild desert region of Cave Creek, Arizona, that I was once again startled by what certainly appeared to be the astonishing level of Moses' ability to understand either our spoken language or our transmitted mental images.

I was sitting at my word processor, working very intensely on a book deadline.

Moses was lying behind me, chewing on a toy.

Visualize that my back is to the dog. I am completely focused on my writing. He is extremely focused on his chew toy.

And then it happened. My thoughts began to crumble. I wasn't getting the words I wanted from my brain box.

For the first time I heard Moses chewing. And it began to annoy me just a little bit, because I was losing my concentration; and my senses were registering stimuli other than my internal dictation.

As I tried my best to refocus, to redirect my thoughts, the sound of his chewing became louder.

You remember the night when you were a kid and you finally got to the movies to see your favorite action hero save the western world from evil? Maybe it was Alan Ladd who had this really terrific, menacingly low voice, but who didn't always talk quite loud enough. And there's this totally obnoxious kid sitting right behind you who sounds like he is chewing his popcorn the way a cornered rat would chew its way out of the large cardboard box. And this kid keeps chewing and chewing. And you keep straining to hear every dynamic and meaningful word your hero is saying. But the kid behind you keeps chewing and chewing . . .

So anyway, you remember.

And now I am older and wiser and know in my heart of hearts that Moses is not chewing louder on purpose the way I always suspected the obnoxious kid who sat behind me with the popcorn was deliberately chewing louder to smother Alan Ladd's threats to the Nazis. And I know that it would be wrong to punish Moses for chewing a toy simply because it annoyed me—just as it was probably wrong to pour my soda on the obnoxious kid simply because *he* annoyed me.

Without turning around in my chair, without removing my eyes from the screen of the word processor, I said in what was little more than a whisper, "Oh, Moses, how I do wish that you would find a quieter toy to chew."

The virtually silent request was no sooner away from my lips when Moses got immediately to his feet. He was gone for no more than two minutes; and when he returned to plop once again on the rug behind me, he had brought with him a very pliable, very noiseless rubber toy on which to chew.

Mind you: my back was turned to Moses. I spoke my frustration with his noisy chewing in barely a whisper. And it was a whisper spoken in almost a monotone. More like a long, steady, one-note sigh.

But good old Moses was more than pleased to comply with my request. He had returned with a chew toy in which he had complete confidence that he could chew away to his heart's content without annoying his temperamental daddy's ears.

I guess that I have found that high-level communication with Moses truly works best when I remain calm in thought, word, and deed.

Moses and I go for a long walk every day—rain or shine, sizzling sun or twenty below. Whenever she can, Mother Sherry joins Moses and Daddy, and we can really observe his happy walk. Moses will always watch the door to see if Mama is coming with us, and he will not give up the vigil until I say, "Mama can't come today."

This wonderful nature walk is quite likely Moses' high spot of the day. We always find it exhilarating and uplifting, beneficial to both body and soul; and I am certain that our big Lab discovers even more dimensions to our river walk than we do. We never fail to see deer, squirrels, rabbits, mink, muskrats, and an occasional fox. Crows call noisily to us to watch out for the hawks circling overhead, and blue jays angrily warn us not to walk too close to their nests.

When it is just Moses and I who embark on these idyllic journeys, I really practice getting inside my main man's head. I give such thought-commands as, "Today we take the path to the left" or "Let's loop the pond before we go into the woods," and then watch Moses comply without a spoken word or a visual sign from me.

In her fascinating book, *Animal Talk: Interspecies Telepathic Communication,* Penelope Smith makes a point with which I wholeheartedly agree:

"The more you respect animals' intelligence, talk to them conversationally, include them in your life, and regard them as friends, the more intelligent and warm responses you'll usually get. Beings of all kind tend to flower when they are showered with warmth and understanding from others."

I also found it very interesting that in advising others in how to communicate with animals, Penelope lists as the first step an attitude of calm and the attainment of a peaceful environment.

"One of the major barriers to receiving communication from animals is allowing your own thoughts, distractions, or preconceived notions to interfere," she warns. "You need to be quietly receptive to what animals wish to relay. If you add to or change their communication, you won't really understand them."

I suppose I first observed this truism in a very simplistic way when I was a boy on the farm and was given the chore of herding pigs or cattle. I noticed that if I stayed calm and confident, the herd seemed to walk in an orderly fashion and Queen appeared to be able to read my thoughts: "Oh, oh, watch the roan heifer. I think she's doubling back. Get her back in line. That's right. Good girl!"

If, however, I grew nervous or uncomfortable with my burden of responsibility and uncertain that I could adequately fulfill it, the pigs or cattle started acting spooked. Queen became almost hyperactive, as if she were doing her best to compensate for my feelings of inadequacy. She would begin to snap at the animals, punishing them cruelly for lagging behind or darting ahead.

If I should then begin to shout at Queen, she would become even more aggressive toward the animals. She was responding to the diminishing elements of calmness in my increasingly nervous mind.

If I totally lost it, Queen would revert to a savage: a wild dog, viciously attacking the animals rather than herding them. And, of course, the more I panicked, the more vicious she would become.

And then we had a stampede. Perhaps not on the scale of those you may have seen in John Wayne westerns, but large enough to scatter the pigs and cattle throughout the corn and soybean fields. And serious enough to put both Queen and me in the doghouse for the next few days.

Moses the Talking Labrador

Before I begin detailing exercises that will increase your ability to communicate with your dog, I want to say a few words about those dogs who already speak to their humans. Sadly, I am not able to refer to canines who can actually form understandable human words and sentences. If I were, I would become a millionaire this summer touring county fairs from

Alabama to Alberta. I am, of course, referring to those dogs who regularly mimic human speech.

A good friend of mine had a dog who would carry on lengthy conversations with him:

"Hello, Jiggs."
"Ahh-roo."
"How are you today?"
"Arf-arf!"
"Think it will rain?"
"Ahh-ruff. Ahh-roo!"
"Would you like some chow?"
"Arf! Arf!"

And so on it would go.

In other words, for every verbal question, comment, or greeting directed at Jiggs, he would respond immediately with a vocal sound or two of his own. He frequently engaged in such dialogues with complete strangers, and always with members of his human family. Jiggs truly appeared to be imitating the patterns of human conversation and perhaps even mimicking the words as they may have sounded to him.

His motive? I should think that this was but one of the methods that this intelligent, lively, loving dog employed to create a closer bond with his humans.

I have other friends whose dogs seem to love to sing along with them and with their families during group musicales. Whenever this one elderly gentleman of my acquaintance sits down to tickle the ivories, his little dachshund stands up on his hind legs, leans his forepaws against the piano bench, and lends his lusty howls to the musical presentation. Another friend, who loves to sing selections from her favorite operas around the house, never gets through an aria without her massive Great Dane making it into a duet.

I have joked with Sherry that Moses' mother must have

been frightened by a chimpanzee, for our big black Labrador seldom barks—he "talks."

If there should be someone at the door, Moses doesn't bark to alert us. Such an act of sounding the natural canine alarm system would be too . . . well, primitive and crude. No, Moses comes to us and says, "Uh-uh-uh-mm-mm-uh-uh!" —sounding for all the world like Cheetah warning Tarzan in all those old Johnny Weissmuller movies.

If we should become a bit too busy and neglect to fill his water bowl often enough on a warm day, Moses doesn't whine or bark his complaint. He finds whichever one of us is closest, fixes us with an intense gaze, and with just enough polite emphasis, utters, "Uh-uh-uh-uh!"

Perhaps the ringing of the telephone hurts his ears or irritates him in some way. One ring, and he is at our side: "Uh-uh-uh-uh!" *Please, answer your darn telephone!*

Not long ago, Moses and I were taking our daily river walk on one of those brisk, twenty-below-zero January afternoons in northern Iowa. Because I had my parka's hood tightened around my head, my breathing mask over my nose, and my stocking cap pulled low on my forehead, my normal area of visual perception had been decreased, so when I looked back on the trail and did not immediately see Moses' black bulk against the white snow, I became concerned.

"Moses!" I called. It was so unlike him to lag behind. No deer scent was that tempting. He liked to blaze the trail just ahead of me in the fresh snow. "Moses! Where are you?"

And then I heard, "Uh-uh-uh!" and felt his snout tapping my knee.

He had been beside me all the time. I had been so bundled up against the subzero temperature that I couldn't see him at my side.

I had to laugh at the puzzled expression on his face. "Has Daddy gone crazy with the cold?" he seemed to be asking himself. "He yells for me when I'm standing right beside him freezing my keester off! Maybe we better head back to the house so he can get some rest."

Entering the Silence to Achieve an Attitude of Calm and to Balance Your Emotions

As we have already discussed, until you can achieve an attitude of mental calm and emotional balance, your efforts to attain a high level of communication with your dog will be almost impossible to accomplish. In order to quiet the mind, you must learn, as Sun Bear always phrased it, to walk in balance on the Earth Mother. And if you truly wish to communicate more effectively with your dog, then you must also respect him as a sovereign entity who has joined you as a companion on your Earth walk.

There is, perhaps, no better way of achieving both an attitude of calm and an appreciation for the Oneness of all of life than going into the Silence in the fashion of the traditional Seneca.

As Grandmother Twylah, Repositor of Wisdom of the Wolf Clan, Seneca nation, tells it, in the very beginning the Seneca lived close to nature. The old legends tell of the wonders of nature and of its effect on all creatures and plants.

It was not long before the ancient ones sensed a powerful force that was revealing itself all around them. They called the force, *Swen-i-o,* the Great Mystery.

The early Seneca studied the lessons afforded them by nature very closely and attentively. Nature was, of course, Mother Earth, the caretaker of all creatures and plants; and the Seneca learned that She had set a pattern that all living things must follow. They understood that each Seneca must also find a way to fit into this pattern if he or she wished to experience true happiness.

Through a lengthy process of trial and error, the ancient people developed a series of techniques that assisted them in achieving a more complete and meaningful use of their minds.

In the quiet atmosphere of the forest, they recognized the presence of the Great Mystery. Its force permeated every soul, thus making every soul a part of it. And there existed a marvelous rhythm and flow of nature that blended all creatures into complete harmony.

When the early people were alone with their thoughts, they listened and heard the Silence.

They listened and saw the Silence.

They listened and smelled the Silence.

They listened and tasted the Silence.

They closed their eyes and felt the Silence deep within.

The woodlands became their chapel, their bodies, their altar.

In the Silence, the ancient ones began to communicate with their Creator, and they received peace.

In solitude, they felt their thoughts being guided to a higher level of awareness. The feeling of belonging to nature, of being one with nature, brought them back, time and time again, to be enchanted by the Great Mystery.

Going into the Silence meant communing with nature in spirit, mind, and body. Nature's atmosphere radiated the spirituality of the Great Mystery and provided the path that led the early Seneca into the Great Silence.

The Secret of the Ages revolved around those attitudes and thoughts that instilled a sense of brotherhood and sisterhood with all of creation. Its practice was carried on in solitude with one's own thoughts in direct communication with the Creator. It mattered not when or where such communication was accomplished, since the body was the altar that housed the spiritual light.

* * *

Grandmother Twylah has often observed that it was only natural that the early people should seek these quiet moments alone in the Silence, for it was their first realization of spiritual love.

Spending time in the Silence of nature also helped the Seneca to learn the unspoken languages of the forest inhabitants; and most of all, it enabled them to understand the necessity of living in harmony with self and with nature.

The Seneca accepted the kinship of all creatures and plants of nature.

The Seneca believed that all creatures and plants were equal in the eyes of Mother Earth, each performing its specific talents according to its unique abilities.

Whenever the Seneca fell out of balance with nature, they created conditions of discord. It was discord that caused the illnesses, frustrations, and disasters that visited them.

When the Seneca developed spiritual equality and a life of spiritual balance, they became a mature people of wisdom.

Among her many beautiful teachings of the Oneness and Seneca wisdom, Grandmother Twylah has shared a number of the mental procedures that assisted the traditional Seneca to locate a place in their mind where peace and contentment lived. Here is one of those techniques:

Visualize yourself walking in the woods.

Your feet are plotting a path on the soft, spongy ground. The path is narrow and winds around trees and bushes so that, at times, you need to duck under the low-hanging branches.

Through the clearing ahead you can see a shimmering lake. The sun spreads a rainbow of colors across the rippling surface.

Upon reaching the water's edge, you stand quietly and listen to the lapping surf as it pushes the pebbles back and forth on the clean, warm sand.

To your left is a log that invites you to sit upon its blanket of moss.

You accept the invitation and settle down upon the cushioned softness.

Feel it press against your body.

A breeze carrying the woodland aromas brushes your hair and caresses your face.

Feel the breeze against your skin. Feel it move through your hair. Breathe deeply of the scents, odors, and aromas of the forest.

As the breeze moves through the branches of the trees above you, they sing the songs of nature in harmony.

The Silence majestically weaves its magic spell as it gathers all nature within its fold.

At last, the serenity of spiritual Silence flows into your every fiber, filling them with divine purity.

You listen and hear the Silence.

You listen and see the Silence.

You listen and smell the Silence.

You listen and taste the Silence.

You listen and feel the embrace of the Silence.

Now, peering through your spiritual eyes, you find the real you dwelling within. And as you drift along with the ebbing tide of spirituality, *you and nature become one* in intimate reunion with the Supreme Power, the Great Mystery.

The Seneca taught their children the importance of identifying themselves with all the creatures and the plants of Mother Earth. This was the first step in helping the little ones to recognize the problems that all creatures and plants must overcome in order to stay in harmony with nature.

The Seneca children learned the difference between creatures, but they *felt* the *same spirit* flowing through themselves and through all of the plants and animals in nature.

Forging a Mindlink with Your Dog

Sit down facing your dog. Do not speak.

Look at your dog's face for at least two or three minutes. Even if you feel that you have looked into those beautiful, loving, soulful eyes a thousand times before, look into them anew and search their infinite depths.

Truly become aware of the details of your dog's face. Notice the various colors and textures of its coat. Study the shapes and characteristics of its snout, face, eyes, teeth, and so on.

Is there any aspect of your dog's face that seems to attract you or intrigue you more than any other?

Try to imagine what your dog is thinking.

Try to visualize how *you* look through your dog's eyes.

What aspects of your personal appearance do you think most attracts or intrigues your dog?

Focus on transmitting or receiving a thought-image from your dog.

If you have noticed that your dog has seemed troubled about something lately, try to receive an impression of what it is that has been causing him or her stress.

Or you might try giving your dog a mental command, such as fetching one of his or her favorite toys.

Are there any images that seem to be moving into your consciousness? If so, focus on those images.

As you focus on those images, pay close attention if they in any way make you tense or nervous, excited or anticipatory.

Continue to observe your dog closely. Does he or she seem in any way to be acting tense or nervous, excited or anticipatory? Your dog may be transmitting thought-images of what has been troubling him or her.

Remain silent and still as long as you and your dog can manage to do so. Seriously, and as objectively as possible, evaluate the success of your experiment.

Did you receive what you believe to have been clear thought-images from your dog?

Did your dog respond to your mental command or suggestion?

Did you feel that you gained any new insights into your dog's personality and mental-emotional makeup?

Do you feel that you and your dog created a deeper bond by practicing this experiment?

Achieving Telepathic Transfer with Your Dog

Sit quietly by yourself for a few moments before you attempt this exercise in telepathic transfer with your dog. You might visualize yourself as an ancient Seneca finding a quiet, peaceful place in the forest in which to enter the Silence.

Visualize the vastness of space. Contemplate the measurelessness of time.

See yourself as a circle that grows and grows until it encompasses the Earth, the galaxy.

See yourself blending into a wonderful state of oneness with the Great Mystery.

Now visualize your dog, the sovereign entity that you wish to contact telepathically.

See it clearly. Smell it. Hear it. Feel it. Be keenly aware of its presence.

In your mind, speak to your dog as if it were sitting or standing there beside you. Do not speak aloud. Speak mentally.

Breathe in three comfortably deep breaths. The act of

breathing will help bring power to your mental broadcasting station.

Once again, mentally relay the message that you wish your dog to receive from you. Ask him to come to you. Or perhaps ask him to bring you one of his favorite toys.

Continue to transmit your command to your dog for no more than five minutes. This exercise will produce results, but the time required to achieve success with your dog depends on so many variables that it is best not to tire yourself on the very first attempt.

If you do not accomplish your goal of telepathic communication on the first try, repeat the experiment on the next day —at the very same time, if at all possible. Continue your experiments until you achieve the mind transfer necessary to complete a successful telepathic communication between you and your dog.

The Legend of the White Buffalo Woman and an Exercise in Learning to Become One with All Life

I stopped hunting when I was sixteen. Although I can still be lured out to do some plinking and target shooting, I have not hunted an animal since the day when it seemed as if I had wantonly slain the king of the jackrabbits.

I remember that it was a beautiful day in early spring. The last vestiges of snow and ice had melted into field and forest, and I was feeling very alive and joyous on that sunny afternoon.

And then I spotted him. The largest jackrabbit that I had ever seen. When I had first noticed the critter running across a plowed field, I thought that it was a stray dog. But now that it was coming closer, I could see that it was one big bunny.

As destiny would have it, I had my .22 rifle with me. I

crouched down beside a pine tree and steadied my gun elbow on my knee.

Sadly, it did not occur to me to admire his strength and beauty or to consider that he might really have been the king of the jackrabbits.

Reflecting back on the scene, I don't know why I couldn't have been satisfied simply to appreciate him as another of God's marvelous creations.

To my shame, all I could think of was pulling the trigger.

The .22 hollow-point slug struck home, slamming him off his graceful, loping stride and rolling him hard into a clump of grass.

I worked the slide and moved another cartridge into the breech. I began to walk toward my downed prey, ready to finish the job if he should still be alive.

I was only a few feet from the big rabbit when he arched up on his forepaws, looked directly at my face, and emitted a shrill, piercing cry.

I don't know how that rabbit's scream might have sounded to you if you had been there beside me, but to my ears, the rabbit's death shout was, *"Why?"*

The scream that I heard as an accusatory question reverberated in my brain. *Why?*

And indeed, I had no respectable or respectful answer for having taken his life.

I didn't need his flesh for my food.

I didn't need his fur for my clothing.

He certainly posed no threat to me.

I had taken his life for no other reason than *sport*—that feeble excuse that some of us use to justify the senseless slaughter of other species. Other species that we consider somehow *lower* than our own kind.

And then a most remarkable experience occurred—one which I shall never forget.

As I stood before the dying rabbit, feeling ashamed and

saddened, I suddenly saw *me* through *his* eyes! A skinny man-child in T-shirt and jeans holding a deadly weapon in his hands.

But rather than feeling contempt or hatred emanating from him for my having irresponsibly taken his life, I sensed that what he was truly transmitting to my consciousness was the terrible realization that I had just killed a part of *myself*.

Somehow, in a way that I was dimly beginning to perceive, the rabbit and I were linked together in some larger vision of reality. Somehow he and I were one.

And then it seemed as though I were about to faint as my mind began to spin and reel. As strange as it might seem, I suddenly felt one with the grass, with the pine tree, with a cloud moving overhead. I was a part of everything—and everything was a part of me.

I fell to my knees before the rabbit and began to weep. I begged his forgiveness for my stupid, selfish, savage act.

The big rabbit shuddered and a bright red bubble of blood formed around his nostrils. He lay still and the bubble burst. He was dead. He could not grant me the forgiveness that I required to soothe my conscience.

And then I understood that only I could expiate my sin of senseless slaughter. It was up to me to remain in balance with the Oneness and to forever respect the individual sovereignty of all life forms on the Earth Mother.

Every student of Native American plains culture has heard references to the legend of the White Buffalo. Novels and motion pictures portraying frontier life will frequently include dramatic scenes depicting a native tribe's alleged superstitious awe of the sacred white animal.

Around 1972 or 1973, Dallas Chief Eagle of the Lakota translated the actual legend as it was set forth in the oral traditions of his people, and he was kind enough to share it with me. The story has been repeated to countless generations as a teaching device. The words are both powerful and beautiful in their simplicity, so take care not to block the timeless relevance of their message with the shield of sophistication that modern folks seem to raise when they are exposed to "primitive" myths. Do not be afraid to learn from ancient wise ones who have long ago made their journey to the Spirit World.

This sacred legend had its beginning many winters before the Great Invasion from the dawn country. To ensure its continuation, this legend is always handed down by those whose minds and eyes are wise and kind, those acquainted with sacred chants and meditations.

In an age before we had horses, in a season of budding spring, two braves went out scouting for buffalo. For three days they hunted and tracked over plain, hill, and valley. On the fourth day, following the sunrise, the braves caught sight of a buffalo herd in a valley on the eastern stretch of the mountains.

The two hunters rushed their descent into the valley and, through habit of many hunts, slowed their pace as they neared the buffalo. Then it was, with equal surprise and joy, that they noticed the white buffalo in the center of the herd. White with fur like winter etching, the prairie monarch stood motionless, enveloped in mystic vapor.

The hunters robed themselves in wolf and coyote hides to hide their human odor and readied their weapons. The buffalo throughout the valley began to move toward the white buffalo and to form a circle around him.

As they crept closer to the herd, the spirit of the white buffalo fully enveloped them, causing them to forget their desire to kill. A blinding white flash brought them up straight, and in place of the white buffalo stood a beautiful woman clothed in complete whiteness.

In sunlit grandeur, she stood before them with hands extended, and the soft whisper of the wind made her hair, white skin, white robe, and white buckskin dress shimmer radiantly. Her mouth moved, and her voice, gentle and warm, flowed with a harmony that brought quiet to the valley.

> I was here before the rains and the violent sea.
> I was here before the snows and the hail.
> I was here before the mountains and the winds.
> I am the spirit of Nature.
>
> I am in the light that fills the Earth, and in the darkness of nighttime.
> I give colors to nature, for I am in nature's growth and fruits.
> I am again in nature where themes of mystic wisdom are found.
> I am in your chants and laughter.
> I am in the tears that flow from sorrow.
> I am in the bright, joyous eyes of the children.
>
> I am in the substance that gives unity, completeness, and oneness.
> I am in the mountains as a conscious symbol to all humankind when Earth's face is being scarred with spirituality undone.
> I am in you when you walk the simple path of the red man.
>
> I am in you when you show love of humankind, for I also give love to those who are loving.
> I am in the response of love among all humans, for this is a path that is a blessing and fulfillment of the Great Spirit.
> I must leave you now to appear in another age, but I leave you with the red man's path.

Complete stillness was everywhere. The White Buffalo Spirit withdrew her hands, and with a glowing smile of eternal love, her body began to turn to vapor.

One of the hunters could no longer contain himself in the presence of the beauty of the White Buffalo Spirit. His mind filled with extreme desire, and he flung his weapons aside, threw off his robe, and rushed for the fading spirit.

A blinding flash again filled the circle. The White Buffalo Spirit was gone; the white buffalo was gone; and all that remained of the impetuous hunter was his skull, his formless bones, and his gray ashes.

This, brothers and sisters, is why we hold the White Buffalo to be sacred. The White Buffalo moves without the threat of arrow or lance, whether we sight him in the northern forest, the plains country, or in the mountain regions.

I hope that you can interpret the deep wisdom of this holy legend, and that you, my brothers and sisters, may help bring its message to all people.

Here is a guided visualization that I have used to help people experience the oneness of all life. You may serve as your own guide through the experience by pre-recording your own voice reading the instructions. Or you may ask a trusted friend or loved one to read the meditation to you and lead you through the experience.

For added power, you might play some appropriate music in the background. Some excellent recordings of Native American flute music have been made available to the public, and these traditional melodies are perfect aids to the overall enrichment of the experience. You may select whatever music works best to place you in a dreamy, drifting mood. Just be certain that it does not contain any lyrics, for they will only distract you from achieving the full effect of the visualization.

Enter a very relaxed state of mind. When you have reached a deep level, when you have gone deep, deep within—moving toward the very center of your essence—begin to tell yourself that you have the ability to visualize the conditions of your own vision quest in search of the spirit of Oneness with All That Is.

Tell yourself that you have the ability to tap into the eternal transmission of universal truth from which you may draw power and strength. Tell yourself that you have the ability to evolve as a spiritual being and to develop the openness of mind that will permit you to communicate with your dog and with all sovereign entities on the planet.

Visualize yourself as a traditional Native American tribesperson embarking on your vision quest.

Perhaps like so many spiritual seekers on their quest, you have found a small clearing in the forest which has a number of rocks of various sizes at one end of the nearly barren area. Remembering that your Medicine Priest told you to tire the physical body with mundane, monotonous tasks, pick up one of the rocks and carry it to the opposite side of the clearing.

In your mind see yourself carrying the rock. See yourself carrying it to the other side of the clearing. See yourself placing the rock down on the ground, then turning around to get another rock.

See yourself picking up a new rock, carrying it slowly to the other side of the clearing, and setting it on the ground.

Then see yourself picking up another rock . . . and another . . . and another . . . carrying each one slowly to the other side of the clearing. Back and forth, over and over again.

Know and understand that you are performing this task for the sole purpose of depleting the physical self with monotonous exercise.

Know and understand that you are distracting the conscious mind with dull activity, that you are doing this to free the real you within, so that it can soar free of the physical body.

Now feel your body becoming very, very tired.

Your body is becoming very, very heavy. It feels very, very dull.

You have no aching muscles or sore tendons, but you are very tired. Your physical body is exhausted and in need of rest.

See yourself lying down on a blanket to rest, to relax.

With every breath you take, you find that you are becoming more and more relaxed.

Nothing can disturb you; nothing can distress you. Nothing can trouble your mind.

No sound can distract you. In fact, any sound that you might hear will only help you to become more and more relaxed . . . more and more at peace.

Slowly you become aware of a presence near you. As you look up, you see a large, bluish white light moving toward you from the forest.

You are not afraid, for you sense a great spiritual presence approaching you.

As you watch with great expectation, the glowing, bluish white light begins to assume human form.

As the light swirls and becomes solid, you behold before you the image of the White Buffalo Woman.

Hear her words as she speaks to you:

> "I was here before the rains and the violent sea.
> "I was here before the snows and the hail.
> "I was here before the mountains and the winds.
> *"I am the Spirit of Nature.*
> "I am in the light that fills the Earth.
> "I am in the darkness of nighttime.
> "I am in the substance that gives unity, completeness, and oneness."

The holy White Buffalo Woman smiles benevolently, then bends over and touches your shoulder gently. The Holy One's forefinger lightly touches your eyes, your ears, then your mouth.

You know within that this touching symbolizes that you are about to see and to hear a wondrous revelation, which you must share with others.

You feel totally at peace and relaxed. You feel totally loved.

The White Buffalo Woman is showing you something very important. Stretching before you is something that appears to be a gigantic tapestry that has been woven of multicolored living lights, lights that are pulsating, throbbing with life.

The energy of the Great Mystery combines with the medicine power of the White Buffalo Woman, and you are being made aware that you are *becoming one with the great pattern of all life*.

In a marvelous, pulsating movement of beautiful lights and living energy, your soul feels a unity with all living things.

You see before you now a *plant*—any flower, tree, grass, or shrub.

Become one with its essence.

Become one with its level of awareness.

Be that plant.

Be that level of energy expression.

Now see before you an *insect*—any insect, crawling or flying.

Become one with its essence.

Become one with its level of awareness.

Be that insect.

Be that level of energy expression.

See before you now a *creature of the waters*—any creature that lives in sea, stream, lake, or pond.

Become one with its essence.

Become one with its level of awareness.

Be that creature of the waters.
Be that level of energy expression.
See before you a *bird*—any flying creature of the air.
Become one with its essence.
Become one with its level of awareness.
Be that flying creature of the air.
Be that level of energy expression.
See before you now an *animal*—any animal that lives on land or in the sea.
Become one with its essence.
Become one with its level of awareness.
Be that creature of land or sea.
Be that level of energy expression.
See before you another of your own kind—a man, a woman, young or old.
Go into that person.
Become one with that person's essence.
Become one with that person's level of awareness.
Be that person.
Be that level of energy expression.
See now the image of your dog—your loyal, loving four-legged brother or sister.
Focus upon its beauty, its strength, its endurance.
Become one with its essence.
Become one with its level of awareness.
Be one with its love.
Be one with that level of energy expression.
And now the White Buffalo Woman is telling you that you forever bear responsibility for all plant and animal life.
You have become one with all things that walk on two legs or four, with all things that fly, with all things that crawl, with all things that grow in the soil or sustain themselves in the waters.
At this eternal second in the energy of the Eternal Now, at this vibrational level of oneness with all living things, at this

frequency of awareness with the Great Mystery, the White Buffalo Woman gives you her blessing and leaves her human shape to become once again the globe of bluish white light.

When you return to full waking consciousness at the count of five, you will feel morally elevated. You will feel that your spiritual essence is immortal. You will feel illumined, enlightened, at one with all living things.

When you awaken at the count of five, you will feel better and healthier than ever before in your life.

You will awaken at the count of five, filled with knowledge, filled with wisdom, filled with love.

One . . . coming awake, feeling very good.

Two . . . coming more and more awake, filled with wisdom and knowledge.

Three . . . coming wider awake, filled with love.

Four . . . wider and wider awake, feeling oneness with all living things.

Five . . . wide awake and feeling great!

TWELVE

Ghost Dogs—
Do They Prove Survival?

I could not have been more than three or four years old on that sunny summer's day when I spotted a cute little man with a Lone Ranger mask over his eyes crawling into a burrow. Quite naturally, I decided that I wanted to pay the mysterious and intriguing fellow a visit.

Iowa is next door to the Badger State of Wisconsin, but in those days (1939–1940), the Hawkeye State had its share of the feisty furballs with the Lone Ranger masks. And as any reasonable person of any outdoors experience will quickly inform you, you do not want to mess with a badger. And you most certainly do not crawl into his burrow without an invitation—which you will not get unless you happen to be a badger of the opposite sex.

But since I was under the age of five, I had not attained either the requisite outdoors experience or the onset of reason that would have prevented me from trying to crawl in the burrow after Mr. Badger.

I can remember the perturbed fellow letting me know in no uncertain terms that I was an unwelcome, uninvited guest in his domicile, but I know that he did not bite me. Knowledgeable folks have since told me that I would not forget a badger bite. I remember his snarling and raising a fuss at me, and I have a graphic recollection of his deciding to set out after me to teach me a good lesson.

I have always had good endurance, but I have never been a fast runner—even with a badger, a bull, and once a bear close behind me. I am certain that my plump little legs could not have outdistanced the belligerent badger for very long, and I undoubtedly owe the fact that I am sitting in front of a word processor writing about the incident fifty-five years later to the timely intercession of Bill, our collie.

Now here is the thing that has puzzled me for years. Bill was getting up in years. I don't think he had enough teeth or muscle left to fight off a badger. I have no doubt that he would have given his life for me, but his heroic, unselfish sacrifice would not have been enough to have kept the bellicose badger from finishing me off as well. I can clearly remember Bill engaging the masked marauder in what would certainly have qualified as mortal combat, and I did have enough reason to envision Bill's inevitable fate and to begin to cry in fear and sorrow. *But I cannot remember where the other two dogs suddenly came from.*

Two long, lanky, lop-eared hounds were there, backing up Bill, giving the badger what-for, until he wisely decided to scamper in retreat toward an old pine tree and seek refuge in a branch just high enough to avoid the snapping teeth of the dogs.

Given fresh courage by the canine reinforcements, I threw a couple of stones at the badger, both of which fell far short of their target.

Then, having released my anger and humiliation, I took advantage of my adversary having been treed by three big dogs to head for home as fast as those plump little legs would carry me.

But I have always wondered just where those hounds had

come from. We never owned any dog other than collies or shepherds, and a couple of little rat terriers.

And we *never* owned more than one dog at a time. My father had a hard-and-fast rule that we never violated: *One farm, one dog.* It was his firm belief that to own more than one dog was to invite trouble of the worst kind. Two or three dogs would be more easily tempted to form impromptu hunting parties and slaughter the very livestock they were supposed to be protecting.

To my recollection, no neighboring farmer owned any dogs that resembled these lanky, long-eared, baying hounds.

Were they strays that just happened to come on the scene and jumped into the fray to give old Bill a helping hand?

If so, they were unthanked heroes, because I never saw them again.

They didn't come back to the farmyard with Bill.

They didn't head for the barn to help themselves to a well-deserved bite to eat from the feed sacks and slop pails.

They seemed to disappear as quickly as they'd materialized.

Had they been my guardian angels in canine disguise?

Or had they been ghost dogs from some other dimension of reality?

In the summer of 1971, my friend Glenn McWane and I conducted a psychic safari employing the remarkable paranormal talents of the famous Chicago sensitive, Irene Hughes. Our experiments consisted primarily of locating houses or locales that were known to have a history of ghostly phenomena, then bringing Mrs. Hughes to the place to see how much data she could acquire about the events which had occurred in those haunted environs. She had been doing extraordinarily well, but on this one occasion she startled us by sighting a ghost dog before we had even reached our designated location.

According to local historians, there was a deserted house in the rural area near Columbus Junction, Iowa, where, in the 1920s, a local resident of dubious reputation had been beaten to death by thugs who worked for Chicago ganglord Al Capone during an argument over liquor manufactured in a still kept on the place. Although the body has never been found, most of the contemporary accounts of the murder pinpointed the house's basement as the corpse's resting place.

The weathered old wooden house that our party approached that night had been one of the retreats that Capone had maintained for himself and his men in tranquil Iowa where they could temporarily escape the rigors of controlling a criminal empire on the tough streets of Chicago.

Suddenly Irene Hughes broke the eerie silence: "I see a large white dog ahead of us."

The three men who were guiding us to the gangsters' old hideaway chorused that they saw nothing.

"I saw him for just a moment up there where those two trees nearly meet over the trail to the house," she said, certain of her sighting of the dog.

I told her that I could see no dog ahead of us, and everyone else agreed that there was no big white dog on the trail.

After a few minutes of discussion, a consensus was established that Irene must have seen a phantom dog.

"See if you can pick up anything more about that dog," one of the men accompanying us asked.

As we passed between the two trees where Irene had seen the large white dog, she spoke intensely: "There's death here! *There's a body buried or hidden right here!*"

Remember that Irene Hughes had absolutely no prior knowledge of any of the houses that we visited on our psychic safari. In most instances, Glenn McWane and I had no more prior knowledge of a haunted site than Irene had. In this particular case, Glenn had learned that local folklore had it that a man had been killed while dealing with Al Capone's bootleggers and that a still had been maintained in a shed on the estate during the late 1920s. But not even a hint of this local legend had been suggested to Irene—yet she kept feeling death in the spot where she had seen the big white dog.

Although she picked up on a host of details that later checked out as being one hundred percent accurate, we didn't locate the actual missing body.

"I know the men who guided us there thought the man was buried in the basement," she said. "But I did not feel a body down there. The only place I felt I was stepping on a body was that tree where the roots were showing. Right where I saw the big white dog. That's where I said, 'I feel death!'"

Later, we did learn that the murder victim had owned a large white wolf and that both the man and his animal had disappeared at the same time. While most local history buffs favored the body-in-the-basement hypothesis, others argued that the corpse had been dumped down an old cistern in back of the house. It was at the site of the cement-covered cistern that Irene kept seeing the big white dog.

Glenn and I found it interesting to speculate over the fact that she saw the spectral wolf at the same spot where she insisted the bootlegger's body lay buried. Perhaps, we theorized, the spirit of the big wolf-dog was still keeping vigil over his master's body, just as it had in life.

In his intriguing and well-documented book, *Pet Souls: Evidence that Animals Survive Death,* author Scott S. Smith recounts numerous stories of men and women who saw the ghosts of their own physically deceased dogs or the spirit forms of canines unknown to them.

"From 1991 to 1993 I asked readers of a couple of dozen magazines about animals and the supernatural to send me any experiences they might have had which would have bearing on this question [of animal immortality]," Smith writes in his Preface.

"I was impressed by the variety and complexity of the reports. Skeptics who believe that such things can be dismissed as wishful hallucinations will be surprised at the collective strengths of these stories. Often the animals seen or sensed are not the most beloved family pets, or they may not have even belonged to the witness. There are also cases of multiple observers. . . . It is difficult to shake the conviction that the deceased pets which were encountered were in some form really there."

Smith recounts the experience of I. L. Heiberg of Wisconsin, who told of the story of Trusty, a German shepherd who lived with his family for fourteen years. It was with great sadness that the Heiberg family was forced to euthanize the old dog when they moved to Portland in 1941.

During the spring of 1945, when they were visiting in Wisconsin, they decided to stop by their former home. Heiberg said that he was sitting in his father's pickup truck when he looked out the side window and saw the image of Trusty, "as plain as could be."

According to author Smith's correspondent, he saw the German shepherd "with her tail wagging and her front feet on the truck running board, looking up at me with a big doggy welcoming grin on her face."

Mindful that his mind and his memories might be playing tricks on him, he looked ahead out the windshield, then back again to the running board—but Trusty was still there.

When Heiberg went to tell his mother of his sighting, he learned that his brother had also claimed to have seen Trusty. He said that the German shepherd had "bounded towards him with a happy grin on her face, tail wagging."

His brother had seen Trusty as transparent, and he had asked their mother to keep his sighting a secret between them. But when the two men compared notes, neither could accuse the other of being crazy.

"I was thirty-one at the time," I. L. Heiberg stated, "and my brother was twenty-nine, so we were old enough to be certain of what we saw."

Iowa's Dark Lady of the Snows and Her White Collie

I first heard this tale of a phantom woman and her ghost dog many years ago from an elderly Iowa farmer who claimed to have had a personal encounter with the mysterious pair on a cold winter's night when he was just a teenager. I'll repeat the story now as closely as I can to the way eighty-year-old Fred McPherson told it to me:

> It was a bitterly cold night in January of 1913 when I was awakened from my sleep by the sounds of heavy feet stomping across the wooden porch. Then a big fist started pounding on the door, and I heard Pete Jensen yelling at me to open up.
>
> I turned up the wick of the lamp beside the bed, slid my feet out from beneath the covers, and gingerly touched my toes to the cold plank flooring. I was going on seventeen when our neighbor Pete Jensen hired me to do his morning and evening chores and look after his place while he was away on a cattle-buying trip. I had not expected Pete to come home for another night at least, but there he was, pounding at the door, wanting to be let into his house.
>
> I quickly pulled on my overalls, then walked barefoot across the rough flooring to open the door for the cold and impatient man.
>
> We spent a few minutes discussing Pete's luck at the mar-

ket, then I laced up my shoes and told him that I might as well head on home.

Pete argued that since it was so late, I should stay the night. "It's cold out there, Fred, and it's already past ten o'clock. Stay here until morning."

I told him that it wasn't that cold and it wasn't too far to walk home. And I knew full well that Pa had been missing me during our own morning and evening chore times.

Pete gave me my wages when he saw it was no use arguing with me, and I set out for our farm, just a little over two miles down the road.

There was a beautiful full moon, and freshly fallen snow lay deep. That bright moon on the smooth snow made the night nearly as light as day. And because it was so clear that night, I decided to take a shortcut across the fields and past an old abandoned farm rather than follow the gravel road.

It was just as I approached the deserted farmhouse that I saw the tall woman dressed in black standing about ten yards ahead of me. Beside her stood a huge white collie.

I could not believe my eyes. No woman I knew would be outside walking around in the bitter cold at that time of night. She was no neighbor woman. I knew everyone for miles around.

I got a real uneasy, eerie feeling. The woman shifted her weight slightly, and I saw that she was carrying a bundle wrapped in some white material.

Her left side was turned toward me, and she seemed to take no notice of my approach. I stopped and watched her. I kept thinking that maybe she would speak up and say something. I mean, like maybe she was in some kind of trouble and needed help.

I was not really scared until that big collie took a couple of steps toward me, and I saw that his eyes seemed to be glowing bright red. That's when it really hit me that I was all alone out here late at night with a mysterious woman and a really strange kind of collie.

Suddenly the tall, dark lady moved away from me; and after she had walked for about twenty yards, she just seemed to disappear in a thicket that grew on a rocky knoll maybe five or six rods from where I first saw her.

Her big collie with the red eyes stayed there watching me for what seemed hours before he, too, followed his mistress into the thicket and disappeared.

Part of me wanted to run back to Pete Jensen and accept his offer to spend the night there. But I made a wide detour of the thicket and continued on my way home in spite of the spooky experience.

The next day, I took a close friend of mine with me and we went back to the place near the abandoned farm where I had seen the tall, dark woman and her white collie with the red eyes. Although we searched the spot for nearly an hour for clues or for footprints, we found nothing. All that we could see were my own footprints in the freshly fallen snow. The dark lady and her red-eyed collie had left no tracks at all.

Later, after I had summoned the courage to tell others of my eerie experience, I learned that several neighbors down through the years had seen the Dark Lady of the Snows and her big collie as they had passed the deserted farm on a cold winter's night. Some said that she was the ghost of a farmwife who had been burned to death in the fire which had gutted the interior of the abandoned farmhouse sometime in the late 1880s. According to the same folks, the ghost dog was that of her devoted collie who had perished in the fire while trying to save her.

I never saw the Dark Lady of the Snows again, and I guess through the years I have always felt kind of privileged that I got to meet two ghosts face to face.

The Ghost of a Big Labrador with Luminous Golden Eyes

A woman, whom she identifies only as "Becky," told writer Ruth Hein that when you live in a house for a time, you develop a feel for the place. "Or maybe you feel a presence there. Sometimes it takes the form of a person, sometimes the form of an object or animal."

According to the account in *Ghostly Tales of Northeast Iowa* by Ruth D. Hein and Vicky L. Hinsenbrock, Becky had encountered denizens of the Other Side ever since she had been a child. Always, though, these entities presented themselves as humans.

It was when Becky and her family moved to a house north of Decorah, Iowa, that the "strange presence" took the form of a dog.

By then, Becky had two sons. When Jimmy, her older boy, had been only about a year old, he was already speaking a few words, one of which happened to be *puppy*—which he applied to any dog, regardless of age or size.

Jimmy would wake up in the night shouting, "Puppy!" Sometimes Becky would hear him in the daytime, scrambling up the stairs from the first floor, yelling that a puppy was after him.

One night, Becky allowed little Jimmy to sleep in her bed. When she heard her younger son crying, she decided to let him sob a little rather than wake Jimmy by getting out of bed. It was, of course, her earnest hope that the baby would fall back asleep.

But he didn't.

She knew that she must get out of bed and go check on him.

Becky sat up, and "there at the end of the bed was a huge black Labrador," staring at Jimmy with "luminous golden eyes."

Becky told Ruth Hein that the strange dog's eyes were more than just bright or shining: "Some weird kind of light seemed to be coming out of them right toward Jimmy. They projected an expression of evil intelligence."

Prompted into action, Becky kicked hard at the dog. "And just that fast, it was gone."

She insists that the creature was there. It was the biggest Labrador that she had ever seen.

"In that one close look in the dim light from the hall, I saw its ears hanging close to its head. I saw the long, powerful jaws and its black, dense coat—and those penetrating gold eyes."

Strangely enough, Jimmy never said *puppy* again to let her know that he had seen the ghost dog. He never even seemed to dream about it. The mysterious entity appeared to have left them for good.

Later, when Jimmy was older, Becky discussed the eerie visitation of the ghostly black Labrador with him. She asked him if he had ever seen it again, and he replied that he had not.

Gratefully, Becky concluded that in the years that followed, Jimmy was never again dogged by the ghost of the big, golden-eyed Labrador.

THIRTEEN

One Brief Moment in Time—Seven Wonderful Years with Sheila

Sandra J. Radhoff of Rio Rancho, New Mexico, told me that it always bothers her to hear someone say that animals don't have spirits. Sandra, an author and publisher of *The Universalian Newsletter,* has included channeled messages in her book *The Kyrian Letters: Transformative Messages for Higher Vision* (Heritage Publications, 1992) that are devoted to pets and the spiritual energies contained within the animal kingdom.

In reflecting upon her marvelous years with Sheila, a German shepherd, Sandra recalled how the dog who would grow to mean so much to her had come into her life:

"In the early autumn of 1975, my young daughter and her stepfather were bicycle riding in our neighborhood in Huntsville, Alabama. I had gone to visit my next-door neighbor. When I returned, my family was sitting in the living room waiting for me. Lying on the floor beside them was a large German shepherd dog, whose paw was bleeding all over the gold carpet."

The next day, Sandra drove the beautiful dog to a veterinarian to have her wounded paw treated. Later, at the grocery store, she purchased cans of dog food and some bones.

"She was such a loving dog that I grew attached to her very quickly and really wanted to keep her. We decided we couldn't do that until we had made an effort to find her owner, so we placed an ad in the local paper, providing all the necessary information."

The day Sandra's "found" ad appeared in the paper, the German shepherd owner's "lost" ad was printed directly beneath it in the same column. That evening they received a call, and the dog's owner, a young man in his twenties, came to their home to see if the dog was indeed his.

"I hoped she wasn't his; but deep down, I knew. The minute he walked through the door to our home, the German shepherd made it very clear that she belonged to him. Her name was Buffy, and she was so very overjoyed to see him."

The young man kept telling Sandra and her husband how much he appreciated their taking such good care of Buffy. He insisted upon paying her veterinarian bill, but they wouldn't let him.

As she packed up the cans of dog food, Sandra told the young man how much she had enjoyed having Buffy around and how much she would miss her. He understood.

"I plan on breeding Buffy," he said. "And if she ever has puppies, I'll give you one because of the care that you gave her."

Sandra was fully aware of the transiency of promises made in the moment and then forgotten with the passage of time. As the weeks passed, the family went on with their lives; and her few days with Buffy slipped deeper into her memories.

Then one day late in the spring of 1976, there was a knock at their front door. Sandra opened it, and there stood Buffy's owner.

"Do you remember that German shepherd dog that you

helped last year?" he asked her. "Well, she had puppies, and I have one for you."

Sandra went out to his car, and there in a little box was the cutest German shepherd puppy that she had ever seen.

"She was only eight weeks old, but ears that seemed far too big for her tiny body stood straight up. Sometimes German shepherd puppies must have their ears taped so they are able to remain straight. Such would not be the case with this dog. She was light tan with dark markings and was blessed with the most beautiful brown eyes. She immediately stole my heart, and I always thought of her as a reward for a good deed—and as a precious gift from Buffy and her young owner."

They named her Sheila, and Sandra remembers that puppyhood was not easy for the little German shepherd, for she possessed a very mischievous nature.

"She forced everyone in the neighborhood to retrieve their Sunday papers early in the morning or else they would end up shredded on my lawn—much to my embarrassment. She was so joyous, however; and when she would look at me with her big, brown eyes, I couldn't stay angry very long.

"As she grew up and became a mature lady, she was loving, gentle, and loyal. She never ceased to be one of the most treasured gifts in my life."

Sheila loved to run, and when the family moved to Colorado, she delighted in camping in the mountains with them. It was around Christmas in 1982 that Sandra noticed that Sheila was limping.

"The problem didn't go away, so I took her to a vet about a month later. His diagnosis indicated that she needed surgery on a ligament in one of her back legs. I decided to have it done, regardless of the cost, because Sheila loved to run."

The surgery appeared to be successful, and Sheila seemed to be healing well. However, one evening as Sandra was rubbing her neck, she felt that the dog's lymph glands were swollen.

She took Sheila back to the veterinarian, and he put her on antibiotics.

"This did no good. The vet began a series of tests on the lymphatic system and blood."

When the test results were in, Sandra was saddened to learn that Sheila had cancer—and it had spread throughout her entire system.

"Sheila developed edema in her hind legs, and she ate little. The vet said that he could put her on steroids, but it would give her only a bit more time.

"As I looked at this beautiful and beloved friend, I knew that although she never made a sound, she was suffering. I knew that her quality of life would never be the same again.

"Making the decision to have her put to sleep was the most difficult and painful thing I have ever done."

Sandra decided to have it done on a Saturday, so her former husband would be home and they would have time to prepare a suitable resting place for Sheila in the open space near their home.

"The decision was made on a Monday, and I spent the entire week with her. I wept a lot that week, and I honestly thought that I would be prepared for her passing by the time that Saturday arrived."

On Friday, June 17, 1983, the day before she had her seven-year-old German shepherd dog, Sheila, put to sleep, Sandra wrote the following short piece dedicated to the memory of her beloved companion:

ONE MOMENT IN TIME

The sun is shining, brightly casting long shadows on the grass. The leaves on the cottonwood tree next door are moving in rhythm with a gentle spring breeze. Birds of assorted species sing their varied songs, and somehow it all comes together in a kind of harmony. A happy squirrel scampers along the power line on his way to the cottonwood tree. Somewhere in the distance there is the sound of someone starting their car with seeming difficulty. Life continuing as it does every spring morning.

Yet, in this routine and peaceful setting, I do not feel a sense of peace. It has not yet come to me, although I wish it would shower upon me and cleanse me from the agony I feel. A beautiful lady is dying to this life, and on the morrow will pass into a higher dimension of life. Knowing all that I know, I am supposed to feel joy for her. And a part of me does. Yet another part of me, a selfish part, perhaps, wants her to stay, wants just a little more time. But then, in the area of loving is there ever enough time?

I look at this moment and somehow life seems pointless. I feel beaten and powerless. A Christ could have healed her. This moment shows me how far I have to go and how powerless I really am. In this world of illusions, so much really is pointless and so much really doesn't make any difference. Maybe it's this truth which caused writer Hugh Prather to say: "And because it is pointless, that truth comforts you and gives you time to heal. But once you have mended, the very futility that gave you rest now impels you to an even greater effort."

The same writer also said: "One has to be devastated. Time and again one has to be torn apart by the facts." Somehow I must believe that from the devastation I feel I will grow and I will learn. If I do not gain from all of this, if I do not learn, then it truly was pointless.

I have watched her slowly moving away from what she was. I have journeyed with her, wondering what she felt and what she thought. Our eyes have met in a kind of knowing. I have touched her to let her know I am still with her and to comfort myself that she has not left me. Yet my agony lies in my knowing that time is running out and that she will journey on with more able masters. In that, I find comfort.

In this moment, I wonder if I will ever find the quality of the relationship we have. Will I ever allow myself to be bonded in love to the same degree? Somehow the loss of her form does not seem so great when I remember the quality of the relationship. I find myself having been blessed with seven years of her presence. It is because of the nature of this love, this all accepting love, that makes me yearn for more time. When life is really good, we don't want change, for we can envision nothing better.

Yet, she must go from this world, and I must release the warmth of her form—although I know I shall never release the memories. And I must go on in the struggles of this world, thankful that our lives came together and together we journeyed for a time. The highest tribute I can pay her is to learn what she has taught and to allow my heart to open once again to another all accepting love. Rod McKuen said of a cat named Sloopy: "Looking back, perhaps she's been the only human thing that ever gave back love to me." In some ways this is how I feel about Sheila. There are qualities within our friendship which surpass those contained in others I have had. In other words, what makes this special is that it is the closest I've been to the exchange of unconditional love. We are simply two life forms journeying in time in acceptance and love for each other's essence. And what in life is better than this?

"On that Saturday morning," Sandra Radhoff recalled, "Sheila appeared to have more energy, and it seemed as though she knew that she was going to leave us. She went into every room in the house, and she would look up and stare as if she could see something that we could not. It was as if she was seeing into the next dimension.

"She willingly got into the van, and we drove to our veterinarian's office.

"The doctor and his wife came out and gave her the injection.

"I didn't think that I had any more tears left in me, but as I watched Sheila leave so softly, it seemed as if I could sense her spirit leaving—and the tears rushed forth again long with the knowing that her energy and her consciousness—everything that had truly been Sheila—had journeyed on, leaving only physical form behind.

"We drove to the place where her physical form would rest and return to the earth—and as we lowered it, wrapped in a linen sheet, into the ground, we both cried."

Sandra said that she found herself in tears on and off throughout that day.

In the months that followed, she would find Sheila's toys or a hidden rawhide bone or a bit of her hair.

"I so longed for her presence. Sheila's vet had told me that I might never want another dog.

"Yet I knew that I could love another dog and there were so many dogs out there in need of good homes. I knew that no other dog could replace Sheila, but I also knew that it was possible that another could have his own place in my heart."

Five months after Sheila had moved to a higher and finer dimension, Sandra opened her heart to a six-week-old Siberian husky named Triton.

"He has been my loving companion for eleven years now," Sandra Radhoff concluded her inspirational account. "The human heart is very expansive—and it has room for many loves."

FOURTEEN

"Fred Is Waiting for Us in Heaven"

I've always thought our daughter, Melissa Hansen, a 1994 *cum laude* graduate of California Lutheran University, to be rather more spiritually conservative than her mother and me so I was quite surprised when I asked her recently if she believed that our dog Moses had a soul. Without hesitation, Melissa said yes.

I suppose that most dog lovers believe that their beloved companion has some spirit or transcendent aspect of personality that will survive physical death, and I am quite certain that those same folks will agree with Patricia Walton of Pennsylvania when she declares that she *knows* that their precious Fred is waiting for them in Heaven.

Patricia recalled that Fred was four months old when, in 1972, with the help of the local Society for the Prevention of Cruelty to Animals, he joined their family.

"He was a little mixed-breed fellow with long bangs that always hid his eyes from clear view," she said. "In those days, our two sons had alternate names that they loved to be called. Six-year-old Terry was 'Terrence of Arabia'; Tim, eighteen months younger, became 'Timothy O'Rourke O'Reilly,' and Fred found himself titled 'Frederick Aloysius Xavier.'"

Patricia said that Fred bore the name well. And as he grew older and more dignified, it seemed always to have been his.

"As silly as it may sound to others now," she allowed, "nine years after Fred's death that special family name can still bring tears to the eyes of at least four people, especially when spoken at their most vulnerable times. To us four Waltons, the name means love and loyalty in their purest forms."

Patricia reflected that the way that Fred loved her and her husband Art and their sons Terry and Tim throughout the life he shared with them "seemed transcendent long before any of us knew the meaning of that word. And the way he disappeared from our lives after sixteen years of intimacy seemed to prove it."

As Fred progressed into ripe old dog age, it seemed obvious that he hated being blind and no longer in control of his faculties.

"Yet the dignity that he had carried from puppyhood did not permit him to whimper to us about it. He carried on as normally as he could; and when he could not hide the evidence of his aging, he tried to act as if nothing was amiss."

Then one morning, the family awakened to find that Fred had disappeared.

"Literally disappeared from inside our home. No doors or windows were ajar. It would have been extremely difficult for Fred to have gotten down the steps into the laundry room and from there into the crawl space under our house—but we searched every corner there anyway, because it was the only possible place where he could be. He was not there. The chain guards were still on the doors."

Not able to believe that Fred could simply have disappeared from inside their home, the Waltons repeatedly searched throughout the house.

Then they undid the chains and went out to scour their yard, the neighborhood, the entire town, looking for Fred.

"We mourned Fred even more, it seemed, than if he had died in our arms, for we could not understand what had happened. We feared that, in some impossible way, Fred had suffered harm."

Impossible?

"Yes," Patricia explained. "It would have taken a tremendous suspension of disbelief for us to believe that some stranger could have sneaked into our home unnoticed by Marcy, our other dog, an excitable little lady who would not have missed the chance to tell us of the intrusion. It really was impossible to consider that some remarkable stranger could have taken Fred out of our home unheard, then relocked the doors and replaced the chain guards from the *inside.*"

Yet even knowing this, the family feared ridicule, and they were not able to tell others what had really happened.

"Instead, we just said that Fred must have run away to die. We even stopped talking about it to each other, because even we couldn't believe what we *knew* to be true: Dogs—or anything else—don't just disappear. They live or they die, but they do not simply cease to exist without an explanation!"

Patricia remembers so many times silently asking Fred where he was.

"Oh, where are you, Frederick Aloysius Xavier? Are you okay now? Where did you go?"

She always had a feeling that Fred heard her crying.

"But the answer that came was in the form of something in which Fred specialized: silence. Our dog Marcy was the 'talker.' Fred was the thinker who sat and watched, seldom voicing his opinions, preferring to show us his feelings by climbing onto the sofa beside us. Sometimes, instead of sitting up next to us, he would suddenly become limp all over and 'accidentally' collapse sideways into our arms—where he often got to stay for a long while. As I said, Marcy always wanted to 'discuss' things first; Fred preferred simply to show us."

Eventually the Waltons got used to living without Fred in their daily lives.

"And then without our sons as they grew and left home to begin their own lives," Patricia said.

In 1989, Patricia and Art discovered that there were other worlds to explore.

"We learned to go within, then to communicate with the discarnate teacher friends we met during our inner journeys. It was an exciting time of new birth for us as we ventured into magical worlds that we had previously seen before only in our peripheral and shadow visions. We found our invisible Master Guides to be *real* in the *realest* sort of way, and they became very important members of our family. Their outpouring of love upon us made us feel more spiritual—and less religious—than ever. The more we discovered of them, the more we learned about the nature of God."

At the same time that Patricia and Art started to become more consciously aware of the spiritual beings who had so long been with them, something weird began to happen to them again—for the first time since their beloved Fred's strange departure.

"We found that when we took photographs, impressions of our guides and other spiritual beings appeared in the light images and reflections," Patricia said.

Acting as their own most severe critics, at first Patricia and Art pretended not to notice the spirit images.

"We pretended we didn't see the face of my grandmother on the windshield of the rental car we drove to the Iowa cemetery where she was buried in 1918. Nor were those other faces those of the guides we had already met—and could thus identify—on the astral plane. After all, we weren't ready to be considered oddballs—or worse.

"Then—just out of curiosity, mind you—we checked some new snapshots once again, *and found Fred sitting beneath what seemed to be the caretaking hands of an angel or guide."*

Patricia and Art were dumbfounded. And yet, they were so relieved.

"Fred was okay—and he'd found a way to let us know it!"

They still don't have any idea how Fred managed to disappear from the inside of their locked home, but now at last they knew that on a higher plane of existence he was healthy and happy—and waiting there for them to join him.

"How like Fred to choose a simple photograph to show us the truth! How like him to want to relieve us of the burden of worry that we had all carried for so long, not knowing for sure where he was. And how like him to use a picture of himself to confirm to us the reality of the beings that we were getting to know and to love."

Patricia commented that she had always said that if things were truly as some fellow churchgoers had said, that there were no animals in Heaven, then she didn't want to go there.

"Now, thanks to many caring teacher guides and spirit friends—and especially to the loving concern of our beloved Frederick Aloysius Xavier—I not only want to go there, I know that when our lessons here on Earth are completed, we will only be returning to our beloved Home—and that our Fred will be waiting there to welcome us!"

FIFTEEN

Saying Hello to Toby Again— in Joey's Body

Beverly Hale Watson, author of such books of inspirational verse as *Reflections of the Heart,* shared the following poignant story of the passing of her dog Toby—and the remarkable return of his spirit in the body of Joey.

For twelve years Beverly and her husband Paul had a black miniature poodle named Toby whom she nicknamed "Shadow," because everywhere she went, he was always at her side.

"We had a bonding between us that was unexplainable," she said. "Toby was more than just a dog."

But one evening when she and Paul returned home a bit later than usual from work, Toby was not there to greet them at the door.

"We began at once to search for him; and when we found him it was evident that something had happened to him because he didn't have the use of one side of his body—nor could he move his head. We suspected that either he had fallen down the stairs or suffered a stroke. We immediately rushed him to the veterinary hospital for diagnosis."

Almost four hours later, Beverly and her husband were told that their beloved Toby had numerous physical problems and a disintegrating spine. Vertebrae in his neck had jammed together, making it impossible for him to move his head.

"The doctor suggested that we take Toby home, and he gave us two choices: One, he could be kept on painkillers for the rest of his life and placed in an area where there were no stairs. Two, we could have him put to sleep. The doctor wanted us to think things over carefully before we made a decision."

Beverly carried Toby out to their car.

"I sensed he knew that we needed to spend some time alone. When we arrived home, I began to receive very clear thought messages from him. He requested that I not lay him in his bed but fix him a place where he could sleep on angle so his head could lie evenly with his body. As I sat next to him, he communicated that he didn't want me to leave."

The next morning Beverly and Paul decided that it was not fair to Toby that he should suffer, so they made the decision to return to the veterinarian's to have their dear poodle put to sleep.

"Toby could move very little, so we carried him inside. As soon as we set him down on the floor in the examination room, it was as if he knew what was going to happen. All of a sudden he began walking briskly around in circles. He had a happy face, and his tail was wagging."

Beverly and her husband left the room knowing that Toby's pain would soon be over. She was also well aware that she would be lost for a while without her best friend.

"Walking to the car, Toby came through to me in thought messages once again. He was free! He was free! He communicated that he no longer had any pain, and he told me to envision him as a lamb leaping over the clouds. As I sat down in the car, trying to hold back my tears, Toby's thoughts continued to give me peace and comfort."

And then Beverly received a most extraordinary message from Toby's spirit: "One day in the future, you will receive a telephone call from a woman moving out of the state. She will not be able to take her one-year-old silver gray poodle with her. She will request that you take him. When the call comes, you are to pick up the dog—for I will be returning to you!"

As an author of spiritually inspired books, Beverly has learned to become attuned to the Inner Voice. At the time of Toby's passing, the following poem was given by spirit to be included in her book, *Reflections of the Heart:*

TOBY

A puppy in black, that's what he was
Who came to our house bringing his love.
His fur was soft, so curly and tight,
His face was so loving, his eyes were so bright.
A handful of fluff, he was so fun to touch!

He christened our carpet, and dined on raw wood
He loved stinky socks and played "catch me" if you could.
He tried our patience with puppyhood games—
Like chewing up rubber mice left within range.

But a smart little fella was he to see
He learned commands with the greatest of ease.
Sit up, lay down, roll over . . . "Oh, please!
"Just give me the treat," he would plead!

As childhood ended, he became quite a teen
He loved to be part of the social scene.
Cats, canaries, and butterflies, too—
Bees in the garden, he'd say, "How'd ya do?"

Ever so gentle of God's creations
Toby engaged in unique conversations

With a pet bird—known as Andy by name—
This dog would speak as though he was same.
Toby would bark, while Andy would squawk
They truly communicated in "animal talk."

As the years did fly by and the children left home
Our once-young puppy into manhood had grown.
His shiny black fur turned to silver and gray
He looked so distinguished in his own way.

A poodle he was, but he didn't know it
Like people, he thought—and even did show it.
A lick on the hand, or curled up in your lap
He shared his love freely, we attest to that.

But fate was to deal him a most discouraging blow
When his spine became crippled, he had to move slow.
He suffered in silence, while enduring the pain
Seeking out comfort that he never obtained.

Our buddy was special, he was a gift from above
Given to us—to care for and love.
But there comes a time when it's not enough
And the Lord calls home His once young pup.

Beverly Hale Watson's creative partner, Cynthia Hyder, handles all the graphics and illustrations of their books. One evening after she had read the above poem, Spirit directed her to get a pad and a pencil. She was to create a portrait of Toby to accompany Beverly's poetic memorial to her pet.

"Cynthia had never seen the dog," Beverly said. "He had died before the two of us started working together. But as she took her pencil in hand, Toby's spirit came through and literally guided her as she drew.

"He informed her of his many physical problems and that

he felt his snout was too short and wide. He had an eye with a blocked tear duct that constantly had matter around it. His topnotch always looked unkempt, but he was proudest of his ears—for they were long and fluffy.

"As she completed the portrait, Toby informed Cynthia that he would sign it—which he did."

Cynthia contacted Beverly the next morning to deliver the picture and to tell her of her remarkable experience with Toby's spirit.

"Needless to say," Beverly commented, "it overwhelmed me emotionally."

One morning in March, nearly seven months after Toby's death in September, Beverly was standing at her kitchen counter when the telephone rang with the fulfillment of his prediction.

"The woman on the other end identified herself and explained that she had been given my name by the Humane Society. She went on to say that she was in the process of moving out of state and due to housing restrictions in her new home, she would not be able to take her one-year-old silver gray poodle with her. She could not understand her feelings, but somehow she just *knew* that I was to take her dog. She wasn't interested in selling him. He was a registered poodle, and her object was to find him a good home. Three people had told her that they wanted to take the dog, she said, but she knew that they were not to have him. Could I pick him up that evening?"

Beverly's first reaction was one of total disbelief.

"I contacted my husband Paul and told him what had happened. We went that night to meet an 'old friend.'

"The owner greeted us with Joey tucked under her arm. As soon as we sat down on the sofa, she put him down on the floor and he went immediately to Paul. Joey jumped up on his lap and wasn't about to move. After exchanging pleasantries and getting information about Joey's likes and dislikes, we departed with the poodle clinging to Paul."

As soon as they arrived home and set Joey down in the foyer, he started checking out the house. Minutes later, he scurried up the stairs, heading for their bedroom.

"He leaped on our bed and quickly tunneled under the blankets to the foot of the bed. That is where Toby used to sleep. As we observed all of Joey's antics the rest of that evening, there was no doubt that Toby had indeed returned."

The next morning when Beverly and Paul opened the back door so Joey could have his morning run, they noticed something very unique about the way he ran. *He moved like a lamb, leaping over clouds!*

"It was an incredible sight to see," Beverly concluded her moving story. "Joey has been with us for four years now. He sticks to me like glue. Although he doesn't speak to me telepathically, he has no difficulty letting me know what he wants. Joey is proof that dogs *don't* die: their spirit lives on."

SIXTEEN

The Weird and Wonderful World of Dogs

I've always known our canine companions to be marvelously adaptable to nearly any kind of situation that we complex and often weird humans can come up with; but I truly got a chuckle when I heard about the two master knife craftsmen of Thiers, France, who cannot work unless their pet dogs lie across their backs.

Alain Grandeponte and Noel Sauvagnat practice their craft at the Cutlery Museum of Thiers, and the handworked knives that they produce are cherished as works of art and valued at more than a thousand dollars each.

However, the men must ply their ancient trade by lying face down on wooden planks that have been carefully placed over huge, moving grindstones. The reason they work in a prone position is so they may apply pressure more evenly when shaping the shafts of metal into valuable knives. In order to keep their back muscles from becoming stiff, a dog perches atop each of the craftsmen.

For twelve hours a day, twelve-year-old spaniel Pomponette straddles the back of Grandeponte and four-year-old spaniel Fanny leans across the back of Sauvagnat. The two patient pooches move slowly higher or lower when they perceive a chill setting in on different muscles.

The two men say that the dogs are like hot water bottles that can move and think.

Without his faithful Pomponette, Grandeponte declared, he knows that he would be suffering rheumatism and other aches and pains, for he must lie in an uncomfortable position for hours at a time, moving shafts of steel back and forth on the massive, moving grindstones.

Sauvagnat agreed that he would be visiting the doctor every week with job-related aches and pains if it were not for Fanny keeping his back in great shape.

Remarkably, the tradition in Thiers of making hunting and table knives over the rotating grindstones—and of using spaniels for mobile, living hot water bottles—goes back to 1472.

Always, the men explained to journalist Janice Gregory, it is spaniels that are used. Not only are they a calm canine breed, but they are of a middle size—not too heavy and not too light. The dogs are selected at an early age and trained to lie patiently for long hours across their human co-worker's back.

Of course the men do take an occasional break, and the dogs take advantage of the time off to romp about outside the museum.

Grandeponte and Sauvagnat said that they were always generous with treats throughout the long day of work, and they took the dogs hunting nearly every weekend.

Down the Hatch!

Some years ago, my wife Sherry took pity on a Lhasa Apso that a couple was about to put to sleep. The reason that they were giving up on him was the fact that he had become so fat that his tummy rubbed the floor when he walked. It was, of course, a shame that they did not see fit to accept their share of the responsibility for the dog's becoming so unhealthily obese, but Sherry took pity on Simba and said that she would take him home with her rather than let him face the executioner.

Confident that with her nutritional background and her interest in health and physical conditioning she would be able to rehabilitate the barely walking, fur-covered bowling ball into a slimmer new doggy, Sherry put him on a diet and managed to whittle Simba down from disgustingly obese to pleasingly plump. Of course that didn't mean that the fuzzy little gourmand did not prove with each passing day that eating was still his favorite pastime, and he had to be watched continually.

Simba was already considerably along in years when Sherry took pity on him and rescued him from the death sentence that his former owners had imposed upon him. He had become quite hard of hearing—except when there were sounds of food being prepared in the kitchen. Rattle a pan and like magic, Simba appeared.

Once when I was making dinner, I wiped my hands on a paper towel and accidentally dropped it as I moved a pan on the counter.

The towel never reached the floor. To my amazement, the ever-hungry Simba, who had been watching my every move as I prepared the evening meal, caught the wet, wadded paper sheet and swallowed it in one contented gulp.

Fearing that the little dog would surely choke on such a large paper towel, I got down on my knees and pried open his mouth with my fingers, hoping to catch the tail of the towel and pull it out of his throat.

There was not a trace of the towel to be seen. It had cleared Simba's teeth and throat and been immediately pulled down to his gullet.

Not only was he not choking or gasping at any kind of impediment lodged in his throat, his tail was wagging happily, as if asking for another helping of soggy towel à lá Brad. None the worse for wear, Simba impatiently awaited the serving of his more traditional dinner.

In our book *More Strange Powers of Pets,* Sherry and I recounted the stories of a Labrador-Newfoundland-mix puppy that swallowed a nine-inch carving knife; a Border collie that gulped down a twelve-inch cake knife; a Great Dane that gobbled down the cue ball from a pool table; and a sixty-pound guard dog that downed a $15,000 diamond ring.

In the summer of 1994, I learned of Darwin, a sad-eyed beagle, who had swallowed his owner's engagement ring.

Becky Davidson said that she had never taken the ring off her finger since her fiancé Rick Ellstrom had placed it there. But on this one occasion, she had taken it off for just a moment and placed it in her shirt pocket. And then a few minutes later when she wished to return the symbol of love to her finger, horror of horrors! It was not in her pocket! As if she had tempted Fate by removing it just that one time, Rick's engagement ring had disappeared.

After she had conducted a thorough search of the area where the ring would have fallen from her shirt pocket, her woman's intuition told Becky that Darwin, her twelve-week-old beagle puppy, had something to do with the ring's mysterious disappearance.

An x-ray at the veterinarian's confirmed Becky's hunch. Darwin had spotted the shiny object on the floor and had obviously decided that it was meant to be a special treat for extra good beagles such as himself.

Becky and Rick stuffed Darwin with high-fiber puppy biscuits in order to help move his digestive process along. Within a couple of days, Darwin passed the ring—and after a good cleaning, it was as good as new.

* * *

When Abby, a one-year-old golden retriever, swallowed a rubber ball, it looked as though she truly had bitten off more than she could chew.

Rita Fisler was out walking her own dog in her neighborhood in Boston when she saw a friend, Mike Gorman, kneeling beside Abby, a normally energetic canine, who was lying still on the ground.

A distraught Gorman told Rita that at first he thought Abby was playing, but then he realized that she wasn't breathing. She had swallowed the rubber ball, and he could tell by the look in her eye that she was dying.

Luckily for Abby, Rita had just completed a CPR course. If those techniques worked for humans, she reasoned, why not for a golden retriever?

She picked up the limp dog and began performing the Heimlich maneuver on Abby.

At first nothing happened, but the determined Rita refused to quit. And then the elated Gorman saw the ball shoot out of Abby's mouth as if it were a cannonball.

Within minutes, thanks to Rita Fisler's determined application of her CPR training, Abby was once again bounding about—and wanting to chase after another rubber ball.

Too Tough to Die

One terrible day in 1990, Donald Ayles of Lynn, Massachusetts, watched in horror as the wheel of a big dump truck rolled over his five-year-old Brittany spaniel Yowser.

Frantically, Donald picked Yowser up and saw that his beloved pal was horribly mangled. His front legs seemed to be crushed—dangling and bleeding, battered and broken.

He remembers that he nearly went berserk, because he so

loved Yowser that he couldn't bear the thought of his companion's pain and suffering.

The truck driver yelled at him to get in the cab so they could rush Yowser to a veterinarian.

The vet wrapped and splinted the spaniel's legs, gave him a tranquilizer, and suggested that Donald take him to Angell Memorial Hospital in Boston for further treatment.

Donald honored the suggestion at once and drove to the hospital to allow the doctors there to examine Yowser. They were optimistic and began a series of treatments designed to restore the spaniel to his full capacities.

Over the next several weeks, Donald took Yowser back and forth to the hospital so many times that he finally hit on the idea of putting the spaniel in a baby stroller so he could more easily wheel him in and out of Angell Memorial. Soon it seemed as though everyone was talking about the spaniel in the stroller and his devoted owner.

The doctor's dedication and Donald's devotion paid off, for in January of 1991, he was able to announce that Yowser was up and about and feeling fine.

Katie Coughlen of Houston, Texas, will never be able to comprehend how anyone could be so cruel as to put fifteen bullet holes in Bo, her gentle, lovable Airedale. And few veterinarians will be able to comprehend how Bo was able to survive this sick act of mindless brutality.

On a pleasant summer's day in 1994, Katie was tending the horse that she boards at a Houston stable. While she directed her attention to the horse, her eight-year-old canine companion, Bo, trotted off to investigate the possibilities of discovery lying in a nearby field.

An hour or so later when she spotted Bo about a mile away in the field, she knew at once that something appeared to be wrong. She could see that Bo was staggering, holding up a paw, and limping badly. As he drew nearer, she saw that he was soaking wet and that he was so covered with blood that his normal tan and black coat appeared red.

While it was obvious to Katie Coughlen, a thirty-one-year-old mother of two, that Bo had gotten wet from the bayou that bordered the field near the stables, it was a terrible mystery as to how he had become soaked with blood.

Bo managed to limp up to Katie, then he collapsed at her feet.

Katie lovingly told him to "hang in there," then she loaded the badly bleeding Bo into her car and rushed him to the nearest veterinary clinic.

The concerned vets quickly deduced that Bo had lost nearly one-fourth of his blood and required an immediate transfusion. An x-ray revealed that someone had shot the Airedale in his front left leg with a .22 rifle or pistol.

Although Bo was covered with small holes and gouges, the veterinarians made a logical diagnosis that he may have received bite marks from a fight with another dog. The bullet wound had probably been made by the owner of Bo's opponent, who shot at the Airedale to scare him off.

On the following day, however, when specialist Dr. Wayne Whitney examined Bo, he was startled to discover that the assumed bite marks were, in actual fact, bullet holes. And Bo had fifteen such holes in his sturdy Airedale body.

Dr. Whitney found that one bullet had passed through Bo's heart muscle. Another had ripped through his chest, filling his lungs with blood. Two slugs had entered Bo's back. Three rounds had shattered a front leg, while a fourth hit a back leg. Eight bullets had struck Bo, leaving him with a total of fifteen holes of entry and exit.

Katie Coughlen declared the bloody violation to be "sickening." It seemed to her as though some demented person had used her lovable Bo for target practice.

Dr. Whitney of the Gulf Coast Veterinary Specialists in Houston told reporter Philip Smith for the *National Enquirer*

(July 5, 1994) that Bo had so many bullet holes in him that it was amazing: "In my twelve years as a vet, I've never heard of a dog being shot eight times and surviving. Bo has a tremendous will to live."

After five days in the animal clinic, the gutsy Airedale was back home with the Coughlens. Other than some arthritis in his front leg, Bo was expected to make a full recovery.

Declaring Bo their "miracle dog," Mrs. Coughlen said with emphasis, "Somebody up there was watching over him."

A nearby neighbor was the human angel watching over Laddie, a German shepherd-mix, and her rescuing the dog from a bullet to the brain has culminated in the three-legged canine's appearance in a motion picture with Nicolas Cage, Jon Lovitz, and Dana Carvey.

Laddie was only a few weeks old when he was hit by a car. At that time his owners were members of a religious group that denies orthodox medical treatment for its human members as well as for their animals, so the pup was forced to languish with a shattered leg.

When gangrene finally set in, Laddie's owners decided to end his misery with a quick bullet to the brain.

Laddie's current owner, Lorne Kerr of Elora, Ontario, said that the dog's guardian angel appeared in the form of a neighbor lady who halted his execution and took him to a veterinarian.

The German shepherd's leg had to be amputated, but Lorne thought there was nothing wrong with a three-legged dog, so the woman gave Laddie to him.

Five years later, in February of 1994, Lorne and Laddie, whom he had nicknamed "Tripod," were enjoying a moonlight stroll when they happened upon a movie crew shooting a scene for *Trapped in Paradise*.

Writer Bob Burns quotes director George Gallo recalling his first sighting of Lorne Kerr and Tripod: "I saw this silhouette of this man with a cap walking his three-legged dog in the snow. It was poetic. I thought, 'Wow! This guy really loves his dog. I've got to put the pup in the movie.' "

Although there were no scenes in the working script that required the appearance of a dog—four- or three-legged—Gallo ordered Laddie written into three scenes.

Lorne Kerr was amused—and a bit amazed—by the whole dazzling series of events. Laddie's formal training consisted of sitting and shaking hands. But that first night of shooting, Laddie performed like a seasoned actor. In fact, he was so good that additional scenes were written for him.

And Lorne is the first to agree that his buddy Tripod deserves to be a star.

Big Mama of Dog Lovers Shares Her Mansion with 800 Pooches

So you think you love dogs. Would you be willing to share your home with eight hundred of them?

Forty-five-year-old Concetta Quattrocchi of Catania, Sicily, gets up at six o'clock every morning to begin the arduous task of feeding and cleaning her four-legged "children," and she stays at her daily duties until midnight.

Concetta is happy in her love-appointed labors, and she is more than pleased to share her twenty-six-room mansion with eight hundred dogs.

Every day, she has to cook about two thousand pounds of food for her hungry hounds.

She admits that such a mammoth grocery bill costs money, about five hundred dollars a day. She has already spent all of her savings and sold her jewelry and unnecessary pieces of furniture. Concetta and her brood survive through donations and the salary she receives from her job as the city dog-catcher.

Recently separated from her real estate investor husband, Concetta has a grown daughter and a son, who, fortunately, is a veterinarian. He visits the estate once a week to check on the health of his mother's canine children. His principal job is to neuter and spay the tenants so the population of the pack does not grow completely out of control.

Concetta's mission of providing a home for stray dogs was realized twenty years ago when she lost her beloved poodle, Pallina.

She had desperately searched everywhere for her cherished pet, for she was well aware of the Sicilian law which decreed that all stray dogs, if not claimed within three days, are put to death or given to laboratories for research projects.

She finally found her dear Pallina in a municipal kennel one hundred miles away. She arrived just in time to keep the veterinarian from putting her to sleep.

But as she walked out of the clinic holding Pallina to her breast, she saw the cages filled with other dogs who would soon be put to death or given over to scientists for medical experiments. The horror of the innocent dogs' fate so upset her that she was unable to sleep that night, and she returned the next day to empty the kennel of its doomed dogs.

Friends and neighbors testify to the fact that Concetta knows each of the eight hundred dogs by its own name.

"They are my children," she told journalist Silvio Piersanti. "It's incredible how much love and warmth animals give you. I couldn't live without them—and they would all be dead if they hadn't had the good luck to run across me."

I should also mention that in addition to the eight hundred pooches, Concetta Quattrocchi also looks after and feeds about one hundred and fifty cats.

"Yo, Wilma!"

Well, after all, they are both mammals. But the romance between eleven-foot-long, two-thousand-pound Wilma the whale and Rocky the husky probably won't last forever, even though, according to Jim Johnson, it was love at first sight.

Wilma, an orphaned beluga whale, first swam into Nova Scotia's Chedabucto Bay in 1993 after her mother had been killed. From the beginning of her sojourn in the bay, she had been very friendly with the local residents; but the minute she set her eyes upon Rocky, she seemed to fall in love.

According to Jim Johnson, a local tour operator, Rocky was on board his boat, looking into the bay, when Wilma spotted him.

"She started circling the boat," Johnson told writer Burt McFarlane. "Then she swam beside us, got on her tail so her head was out of the water, and she was sort of 'standing' there, looking at Rocky. She turned her head from side to side, staring at him with one eye at a time, making clicking and whistling noises out of her blowhole."

And then, to everyone's astonished delight, Rocky leaned out of the boat and rubbed noses and cheeks with Wilma. Since that first "kiss," the two mismatched mammals have repeated their little love ritual dozens of times.

Once, Johnson said, Rocky couldn't resist jumping into the bay to join his whale of a girlfriend.

Wilma poked around at the husky, and he at her. "They seemed as happy as two pups falling over each other."

Although other whales have entered the bay from time to time to come calling on Wilma, she seems true to Rocky; and she refuses to leave the bay with others of her own species.

Johnson concludes that their beautiful Wilma has found a "safe, healthy, and happy home" in Chedabucto Bay with Rocky and the rest of them.

Holy Muttrimony!

A recent survey has found that an incredible 44 percent of women would refuse a suitor's proposal if he asked her to get rid of her dog.

Only 31 percent of the five hundred women surveyed said that they would agree to give up their canine companion if their husband-to-be insisted upon it.

The remaining 25 percent adamantly declared that they would refuse to marry any man who disliked their dog—even if he agreed to let them keep it.

And it is certainly better to declare such strong feelings about your dog before the wedding bells chime than after the squabbles begin. According to a number of legal sources, more and more couples are fighting over custody of their dogs in court, sometimes incurring costs of $10,000 or more.

Roger Galvin, an attorney from Rockville, Maryland, who has handled a number of such pet custody disputes, told writer Philip Smith that we are seeing an increase in these kinds of cases "because more men and women are willing to acknowledge feelings of affection and attachment to an animal."

Louise Oliveras of Miami, Florida, proved so willing to acknowledge her feelings of affection and attachment for her four dogs that she gave everything to her husband in a divorce settlement so she could keep Norton, Ollie, Hughie, and Stanley.

Fifty-one-year-old Louise gave her husband Carlos their $90,000 Miami home, their $100,000 air-conditioning business, a $5,000 income tax refund, and a $3,000 lump sum alimony payment so she could receive full custody of their four bearded collies.

In mid-December of 1993, Louise and Carlos met in divorce court, each demanding custody of the dogs.

In Louise's view, the collies were no more to Carlos than

lamps or items of furniture. To her, the "boys" were the children that she had never had. She said that she would go to jail before she would surrender even one of the dogs to Carlos.

Then, in the third day of the trial, when it looked as though the judge just might award one of the collies to Carlos, Louise saw clearly what she must do.

"I told my lawyer to let him have anything he wanted," she said to journalist Dan McDonald. "The house, the business, the money. All that mattered to me was the dogs."

Dade County Circuit Judge Judith Kreeger, who handled the Oliveras' divorce case, said in the *Enquirer,* January 4, 1994: "It was just like dealing with parents fighting over children. They both claimed to love the dogs and they both wanted to have them. I have never seen a case like this."

SEVENTEEN

The Guardians

Fortunately, I have never been in the kind of harrowing situation where a dog had to pull me from a burning building, protect me from muggers, or drag me from a river. Queen and Reb did face down invisible invaders to our home, however; and I inwardly have never doubted that if the circumstances arose, Moses, Reb, and Queen—and all the other canine friends I have known and loved—would have given their lives for me or my family.

Now I admit that I am basing that conviction on feelings, an inner knowing; and I am certain that any number of skeptics would have no end of sport with my romantic vision of my dogs. At the same time, there exists a large number of well-documented stories of canine heroism and courage from men and women all over the world. Enough, one would think, to make the most ardent doubting Thomas want to run right out and buy a dog of his own.

The Mutt He Rescued from Death Saved His Life

In 1992, when thirty-four-year-old Lee Bellinger, owner of Capitol Hill Publishing Company of Annapolis, Maryland, was visiting his mother in Charlotte, North Carolina, he made the acquaintance of Bundy, a unique black Labrador–pit bull mix. The nine-month-old mutt was about to be hauled off to the pound to be put to death when Lee decided to give him another chance at life.

Lee spent hundreds of dollars in veterinary bills getting Bundy back in shape. The young dog was sick and skinny and filled with worms.

But it turned out that Lee had made an excellent investment.

In January of 1994, he awakened one night to find his room filled with black smoke. Frightened, confused, he tried to find his way to safety.

He began to choke on the heavy smoke; and it was as if he were blind, unable to see a thing, unable to find his way in his own home. He was dizzy, disoriented.

He dropped to the floor and began to crawl. He had to find a way out fast—or he would soon be dead.

Then he felt Bundy brush up against him. Lee reached up, put a finger in his collar, and said, "Let's go for a walk!"

Confidently taking the lead, the big black dog brought his owner to the front door and to safety.

Within seconds, Lee's bedroom was engulfed in 600-degree flames. The two-story house sustained $125,000 in damages from the electrical fire. But both man and dog escaped serious injury.

Bundy had repaid the debt. He had given his benefactor, Lee Bellinger, *his* second chance at life.

Abby Found the Missing Boys When 400 Human Searchers Failed

Three brothers were missing for eighteen hours in the swampy woodlands near Dartmouth, Massachusetts. The oldest was only thirteen; the youngest, nine. How long could they last in the chilling cold and the heavy rain?

What would you be feeling right now if those were *your* kids out there in those dark and cold woods?

Perhaps every single one of the more than four hundred volunteers and law enforcement officials heard a similar monologue repeating itself over and over inside of his or her brain while they desperately searched for the Eklund brothers—Bryan, thirteen; Robert, eleven; and Matthew, nine—on a miserable late winter's day in 1993.

The boys' father, thirty-two-year-old Robert, who had joined the search party, said that the three brothers, their dog, Abby, and their friend, twelve-year-old David Choquette, had been out exploring the frozen marshlands. As David and Abby, who were in the lead, crossed a pond, the ice cracked behind them, preventing the Eklund brothers from following them.

Not to worry, the boys had told David. They would get home another way. They were certain that they knew of a shortcut.

David said that he felt capable of finding his way home, and he and Abby set off on the path on the other side of the pond.

David Choquette and the Eklunds' dog, Abby, a ten-month-old Labrador–German shepherd mix, made it home. Bryan, Robert, and Matthew did not.

That first night, thirty-five volunteers with flashlights searched the dark, swampy woodlands in heavy rain. They were acutely aware that the young boys had no blankets or camping gear with them. They probably didn't even have a match to light a fire. They would be chilled to the bone.

And then the rain turned to snow and made the soft ground even more treacherous.

At home, Donna Eklund prayed for the safety of her sons. They needed a miracle.

Abby probably sent up a doggy prayer of her own, and it is

certain that she became very concerned that her young humans had not found their way home.

When she could not stand to wait or to pace nervously one minute longer, Abby slipped unnoticed out of the Eklund house and went in search of the three boys.

By morning the search party of humans had grown from thirty-five to four hundred, but Abby didn't need any help to find Bryan, Robert, and Matthew. In fact, she found them quite easily.

Just the very sight of Abby raised the boys' spirits. They all huddled around her to pool their body heat, and the brothers were encouraged by her presence. If she had been able to find them, so should the search party.

Abby stayed with the boys until they were found—eighteen hours after they had been reported missing.

Donna Eklund had received her miracle, and her sons were in pretty good condition considering the ordeal that they had been through in the freezing rain, snow, and cold.

As for Abby, well, she was rewarded with a big steak.

Samantha Knew a Little Boy Was About to Freeze to Death

On Valentine's Day, February 14, 1993, Naiomi Johnston of Midland, Ontario, gave birth to a baby girl. And while she was recuperating at a hospital forty miles away, her husband Darryl and their three-year-old son Donald were at home, eagerly anticipating the return of mother with the baby.

Little Donald was so eager to see his mommy and his new baby sister that he thought it would be a marvelous thing to get into his little electric toy car and drive off to visit them in the hospital.

He knew that it was very cold outside, with snowdrifts as high as mountains, so he bundled up as well as he could.

And just in case his dad might possibly object to his setting out to visit Mom and baby sister, he got up really early while Daddy was still sleeping.

Donald's electric car soon stopped moving, its battery run down.

Well, there was nothing to do but to walk. It couldn't be *that* far to the hospital.

Nor did it take Donald *that* long to realize that he was completely lost. And very, very cold.

Constable Kirk Wood of the Ontario Provincial Police told journalist Esmond Choueke that at this point little Donald Johnston was less than thirty minutes from death: "He had no protection from the cold, blowing wind."

But Donald apparently had two guardian angels on duty that cold, cold morning in Ontario—one from heaven, another from a nearby farm.

Farmer Brian Holmes was outside with Samantha, his six-year-old German shepherd, when he noticed that the big dog was acting peculiarly, as if something were wrong. All of a sudden, she lifted her head, sniffed the air, then ran toward the woods.

Holmes finally concluded that Samantha had picked up the scent of a rabbit or some other animal, and he went on with his morning chores.

However, Samantha was not at all interested in rabbits that frigid morning. Somehow she had sensed the desperate plight of a small child.

She found the three-year-old sitting under a tree, cold and crying. She licked his face, nudged him to his feet, and began pushing him in the direction of Holmes' farm home.

Donald threw his arms around Samantha's neck, and she guided him through the trees and eight-foot-high snowdrifts to warmth and life.

Holmes had just begun to wonder about his German shepherd when he saw her coming down the road with a small boy hanging onto her for dear life. The farmer immediately took Donald inside, fed him, and let him get nice and warm.

Somehow, the farmer knew, Samantha had been able to sense that there was a lost little boy somewhere out there among the snowdrifts and the freezing cold. And she had found him and brought him to her owner so that he could save the boy's life.

When Donald's mother heard the news of how Samantha had saved her son from certain death from exposure, she vowed that the German shepherd would never be out of special treats.

Nellie Saves Farmer Trapped Under a Tractor

Seventy-five-year-old Ken Emerson, a tobacco farmer from Vienna, Ontario, was taking a shortcut through a ravine to check on an irrigation dam when the tractor he was driving overturned.

Although it all happened so quickly, Ken remembered being pinned between the front and rear wheels—and then the tractor overturned twice more, knocking him unconscious.

When he regained consciousness, he was flat on his back, pinned beneath the tractor, with a broken leg. He tried to move, but found that he was unable to free himself from either the heavy tractor or the terrible pain.

And then he saw Nellie, his grandson's five-year-old German shepherd, watching him from about thirty feet away. The dog must have tagged along, hoping for some excitement at the dam.

It occurred to Ken that if he could send Nellie home with some indication that things had gone awry, his wife, Pauline, could bring help.

Although it was a spring day, it was still too cold to wrap

his jacket around Nellie and be without its warmth for too long.

Ken finally decided to cut off a piece of his plaid shirt with his pocketknife and stick it under Nellie's collar.

At his first command to "go home," she walked off only about three feet and turned to study the situation. She seemed reluctant to leave him in such a predicament.

Ken gave her three more commands to run home. Still the German shepherd remained at the ravine. It was as if she heard the orders to leave the scene of the accident, but her every instinct told her that her place was at the side of the injured man.

Finally, Ken really "blasted" Nellie, he told a reporter in the July 13, 1993 issue of *Examiner;* and he bellowed at her to *go home!*

"Thank the Lord, she turned, padded downhill, and disappeared downstream."

About ninety minutes later, Pauline Emerson spotted Nellie, wet and muddy, and bearing a piece of Ken's shirt under her collar. Pauline alerted their tenant, Russell Ulch, and a neighbor, Bill Rimnyak, who had a four-wheel-drive truck.

Ken Emerson said later that Bill looked like an angel when he appeared at his side.

Ken was going into shock because of the cold, and he was rushed to Tillsonburg Hospital. There, it was later learned that in addition to the broken leg, he had suffered a broken pelvis, broken ribs, and internal injuries.

Nellie, the faithful German shepherd, had saved the life of her owner's grandfather.

Golden Retriever Blaze Saves Family of Three from House Fire

It may have occurred to the Boyer family of El Cajon, California, to rename Blaze, their golden retriever, something like Extinguisher or Fire Alarm after he saved their lives from a fire that gutted their home in the spring of 1994.

The night before an electrical short started the 1,000-degree fire, little two-year-old Christina had had a bad night. She cried that something was frightening her, so eventually she ended up sleeping between her parents, Don and Judie.

They were all trying to sleep as late as possible the next morning; and then Blaze, normally an extremely quiet, well-behaved dog, began barking in an urgent, demanding manner.

Don Boyer admitted that Blaze was up and down the hallway and to their bedroom three or four times without their taking any particular action other than attempting to fall back asleep. Finally, an exasperated Blaze jumped into the bed with the three groggy Boyers.

At last Judie got up to investigate. To her complete horror, she discovered Christina's bedroom engulfed in flames. Perhaps the two-year-old's budding feminine intuition had alerted her to the fact that there was a very good reason why she should not sleep in her own room that night.

Don made a valiant effort to extinguish the blaze, then made a wise decision to grab his wife and daughter and get out of the house.

Later, a fire department safety specialist told Don that in about another five minutes they could all have been overcome by smoke inhalation.

Ironically, the Boyers did have a smoke alarm, but Don had just taken it down to replace the battery. Lucky for them that Blaze had sounded the alarm instead.

"Blaze is a lifesaver," Don told journalist Charles Downey. "He is a four-footed fire alarm!"

Freddie Pulled Out the Stopper to Save His Owner from Drowning

In August of 1994, forty-nine-year-old Silvana Burnett of Edmonton, Alberta, felt her heartstrings being tugged by Freddie, a five-year-old Maltese–poodle mix, who was about to be sentenced to death. As circumstances would have it, a couple of her acquaintance were moving and had concluded that it would be inconvenient to take Freddie with them. They decided that it would be best to send him to the pound to be put to sleep.

Silvana would have none of that, so she gave the couple fifty dollars and bought Freddie. It would turn out to be the best investment that she ever made.

Just six weeks later, Silvana, who suffers from asthma, was taking a bath when she began to find herself becoming short of breath. In a few more moments, she began wheezing—and then she blacked out.

Helplessly, she slipped under the water in the bathtub.

The next thing she knew, she was spitting soapy water out of her mouth and gasping for breath. Freddie was jumping on her chest, as if to revive her.

The water from the bathtub had been drained, and Freddie's little mouth held the stopper!

The quick-thinking poodle, seeing his new owner, the benefactor who had saved his life, slipping under the water, had jumped into the tub and pulled the stopper out with his teeth.

Courageous Canines Take On All Opponents—Large or Small

When three-year-old Jennifer wandered away from the family

farm near Cowetta, Oklahoma, in October of 1994, her parents, Deborah and Lee Johnson, feared the worst.

All night long, while the Johnsons and hundreds of volunteers searched for the little girl, they could hear the howls of ravenous coyotes echoing across the fields.

The only thing that gave the Johnsons courage was their belief that their loyal dogs, Moose and Muley, were with Jennifer.

The next morning, the searchers gave thanks to God and to the faithful watchdogs Moose and Muley when they found Jennifer safe and unharmed. Evidence indicated that coyotes had encircled the frightened toddler and her two canine bodyguards, but Moose and Muley had not let any of the marauders cross the line to harm their little mistress.

One late winter's morning in 1994, Heidi Kahlke of West Jordan, Utah, was horrified to witness a cougar jump over her fence and land just inches away from the spot where her neighbor's daughter, eight-year-old Becky Briggs, was playing in the Kahlkes' yard.

From time to time, especially during the winter months, hungry mountain lions venture down from the mountains to scavenge food from small towns and villages. The cougar had apparently spotted little Becky playing in the yard.

But before the big cat could lift a paw, Blitzen, Becky's constant canine companion, a ten-year-old Hungarian bird dog, had put a stop to any intentions the cougar might have had of dining on his beloved mistress. Leaping in rage at the unwelcome invader from the mountains, the dog chased it under the Kahlkes' pickup.

Here it was that brave Blitzen kept the cougar cornered for two hours until police and wildlife officials arrived and knocked out the mountain lion with a tranquilizer dart.

The cougar was carted back to the mountains where he

belonged, and Blitzen the brave gained a new neighborhood title, Hero Hound Dog.

Seven-year-old Shaisa Noah had set out on a lovely August day in 1994 on what was intended to be a tranquil nature walk with her twelve-year-old miniature malamute, Lilly.

They had not walked far when Shaisa accidentally stepped on a beehive.

Although she may have attempted to explain her mistake, the angry bees weren't buying any excuses. The buzz was they were out for revenge.

Shaisa had suffered only a couple of stings when tiny, elderly, blind-in-one-eye Lilly selflessly smothered the nest with her furry body.

Because of Lilly's quick and selfless action, Shaisa endured only five bee stings.

And the tough little dog, who suffered stings all over her tiny body, was also pronounced on the mend.

73 Rescues Earns Weela Ken-L Ration's Dog Hero of the Year Award

Weela, a pit bull terrier, seemed to accept a month-long mission to rescue people and animals during the disastrous floods that inundated Southern California early in 1993. The sixty-five-pound, four-legged superhero, winner of the Ken-L Ration Dog Hero of the Year award, was credited with saving the lives of thirty humans, twenty-nine dogs, thirteen horses, and one cat.

Among Weela's heroic deeds were many courageous acts:

- She waded across a raging river to carry a heavy backpack of food to stranded dogs.

- She guided a rescue team around quicksand, thus enabling them to rescue starving horses.
- She sensed a deadly undertow at the edge of the Tijuana River and prevented thirty Mexican men, women, and children from entering the water to cross at that point.
- She located frightened dogs and guided them to high ground.
- She dragged human rescuers free of mud when they were stuck and unable to move.

Weela's owner, Lori Watkins of Imperial Beach, California, spoke of her great pride in her rugged pit bull [*Enquirer,* May 17, 1994]: "Weela was incredible. She hadn't been trained for any type of rescue. She just knew what to do. . . . Once I sank into mud up to my waist. Weela tried to dig me out—then she just grabbed me by the coat and pulled me out! Pit bulls are incredibly strong animals."

EIGHTEEN

We Know Dogs Go to Heaven, Because They're Angels in Disguise

On January 19, 1995, Sherry and I received a fax from Lori Jean Flory of Conifer, Colorado:

"I thought you should know! This evening I saw Stormy clear as day with open eyes. Just in a flash, there and gone; but I *did* see him with open eyes."

The reason why Lori experienced such excitement in being able to see her collie with her open eyes lies in the fact that Stormy died on August 13, 1994.

Although Lori Jean is what some people would call a psychic sensitive and others might label a medium or a channel, she is by no means alone in claiming to have seen the spirit of a dear, departed dog. Because her detailed account of her spiritual experiences during and after the time of Stormy's passing has the potential of alleviating a lot of dog owners' sorrow over the loss of their own beloved canines, I am grateful that she has permitted me to share her inspirational story for this book.

Lori Jean and Charles had no idea that their big collie, Pinewynd's Spring Storm, or Stormy, was ill until they made the move from Aurora to Conifer, Colorado, in June of 1994.

"Stormy had had the occasional problem once or twice a year with a sore throat or even tonsillitis," Lori Jean said. "But he appeared to be his usual bouncy self when we moved, and he seemed to love our new home at 8,200 feet elevation in the Rocky Mountains. It was on July 4, the day our water-pressure holding tank connected to our well in the basement sprang a major leak, that Stormy's previously undisclosed health problems also came to a head."

Charles and Lori Jean were completely unprepared for the veterinarian's diagnosis that Stormy had lymphatic cancer with complications to his heart, lungs, and thyroid, as well as dehydration.

"Stormy was only seven years old. We tried twenty-four hours a day for five weeks to help him, to keep him alive. And when I say twenty-four hours a day, I mean it literally. We were injecting him nearly every two hours with two different fluids. He was also receiving five additional medications, a special diet, digestive enzymes, antibiotics, vitamin therapy, and Bach flower remedies. We monitored his temperature every few hours."

Charles and Lori Jean devoted an entire kitchen counter to Stormy's medical needs. Over the next five weeks, they took the collie to the veterinarian a total of twenty-three times. Stormy had blood tests, x-rays, EKGs, and numerous examinations. Those twenty-three visits cost the Florys about $1,200 in that same five-week period.

"We emotionally and physically exhausted ourselves. Once I spent an entire day holding his paw and cradling his head in a towel. At the same time, we were trying our best not to neglect the emotions of our other three pets. We did everything that we could to try to save Stormy."

On August 13, Stormy communicated mentally to Lori Jean that he wanted to be free of his physical embodiment and the pain and suffering that he was enduring.

"He could barely breathe. His face looked hollow. His eyes

looked dark. He had trouble getting up and walking, and he was no longer able to come to us when we called him. It was clearly time to let him go.

"Part of the reason that we had tried and tried so hard to keep him with us was the fact that he had communicated telepathically with me and told me that he wanted to try to live. Now he was telling me that he wanted to leave the pain behind him and move on to a higher level of reality.

"I have been aware of angels and beings from higher dimensions ever since I was three years old. This may seem unconventional to some people, but I am able to see, sense, and hear spirit beings, outwardly and inwardly.

"Charles and I think that collies—and all dogs—are angels who come to give us love. You see, we believe that collies are highly evolved spiritual beings—individuals with feelings, emotions, and many spiritual lessons to teach us humans.

"We believe that angelic light manifests itself in many, many different ways, not only as beauteous winged beings. Incidentally, angels don't always have wings. They have the ability to manifest in whatever way makes us comfortable so that we may have a relationship together. Collies are but another expression of angelic light.

"Are not all angels messengers of love that God sends to help us grow? We feel so. Look into the eyes of your beloved collie. Look into the soul, and you will see God there, smiling back at you.

"For us to release Stormy was emotionally traumatic. For him, being released from his pain was a gift."

Before the veterinarian put Stormy to sleep, Lori Jean and Charles bent over, hugged him, kissed him on the nose, started sobbing again, and asked him to give them a sign that he was all right.

"We knew he would be, but that moment Charles and I were two emotional wrecks. For us, losing Stormy was one of the most traumatic events we have had to endure."

Stormy told Lori Jean that he did not wish for them to remain while the veterinarian administered the fatal injection.

Later, as the Florys drove home, they were able to feel Stormy's release and relief.

When they arrived back at their house, the "signs" that Lori Jean and Charles had requested from Stormy began at once. For one who is psychically sensitive, such manifestations are a part of her normal existence. From Lori Jean's perspective, she marvels that everyone cannot receive such signs and messages from the other side.

As they stepped into the house, the first sign Stormy gave them was a huge flash of white light where he had lain next to the couch.

"It was where he last lay before our trip to Denver to release him."

The next sign was a picture of an angel that inexplicably fell to the floor.

"One moment it was hanging securely on the wall—the next it was falling to the floor."

That night, Lori Jean saw Stormy's face and white ruff hovering near the ceiling on three different occasions.

"You see," she explained, "in the higher realms of light are special realms where animals go to those beloved angels who care for them. I saw Stormy with a beautiful jeweled collar around his neck.

"When we humans are out of our bodies, we have a body made of light. So it is with animals as well. They are of a group soul, while humans have individual souls."

The next morning, Lori Jean heard a dog bark next to their bed.

"Our other two dogs were upstairs at the time, so I knew what was happening. 'Stormy,' I told him, 'we love you deeply, and you will always be family to us, no matter where you are or what you are doing. We miss you terribly, but we do not want to impede your progress into the Light with our grief. Sweetie, if you are ready to go into the Light now, it is okay. We will always love you.' "

Lori Jean received an impression of strong resistance to that suggestion. Stormy's spirit was not yet ready to leave his earthly environment.

On August 16, three days after Stormy's transition from the physical plane, Lori Jean received the following channeled message as she sat at her computer:

Question for Spirit: Where is Stormy now, and how is he?

His spirit essence is still around you more at this point than it is anywhere else. He is with you everywhere and in all that you think, feel, and do. He is the blowing wind; he is the essence of each leaf upon the trees. . . . He is joyously playful, happy, and energetic. He is out of pain. He suffers no more.

He was experiencing discomfort and pain at the end. What you did, beloved ones, was well-timed. Not too early or too late.

He is well aware of how much you love him, and he loves you even more. Love is eternal, and he is protective of you, for you are his pack, his family, his home. He still considers it to be such. He plays at your feet, and he rides with Charles wherever he goes in the car. Love rejoins with its own, you see. He knows he is missed, and he does not like you to be sad.

"Thank you for caring for me as much as you have," are his words. He is beautiful, shining, and sparkling.

Be free and be love. Release him now and live your life. . . . He wishes for you to send light to his photograph and to keep his pictures out. He lives still.

Lori Jean began to see Stormy—as well as strongly sense him—all around the house. She would catch glimpses of a white light, a face, floppy ears, and a ruff, hovering here, there, and everywhere.

As the days passed, she began to receive inner visions of Stormy. It was clear that he wanted them to know that he was fine.

"One morning I decided, just for the fun of it, to look at the classifieds and see if there might be any ads for collie puppies. I had no real intent of actually obtaining one. I was just looking.

"As I opened the paper to that section, I immediately heard a loud booming sound in the kitchen. I thought, 'Okay, someone is not happy about my doing this.' I knew it was Stormy protesting my thoughts."

On another night, as Lori Jean was feeding their two dogs chopped liver, she heard a loud bark directly behind her.

"I looked at Laddie, our other collie, who was lying in his 'cave' under the dining room table. He looked back at me as if to say, 'Sorry, Mom. But I did *not* bark.'

"I know their barks, and I knew that it was Stormy's spirit, not that of the other dogs, Laddie and Brandy. Stormy had always loved his liver!"

Charles is a letter carrier with the Postal Service, and he began more and more to feel Stormy around him—especially when he was in the presence of grumpy dogs who did not seem to appreciate postal workers.

Charles is also an accomplished astrologer who utilizes the knowledge he acquired in his twenty-four years of teaching astrological classes to provide him with better understanding of the dogs, as well as the people, around him.

"Dogs in general and collies in particular are a joy to live with, show, and have as pets," he said. "Our collies accept and love us unconditionally and are truly the epitome of all-encompassing love. They do not play games. They relate naturally to their energies and their specific personalities, not blocking themselves expressively for one reason or another. It is a lesson for us—to be natural and to be ourselves, just as our collies are."

Charles commented that each individual collie has a distinct personality and is a complex combination of many factors.

Their Laddie is a Scorpio collie, according to Charles, and is usually very calm. Another side of the calm Scorpio personality, however, is a "control problem."

Laddie, a year and a half older than Stormy, was the Alpha dog, the top dog of the Florys' three canines.

"Stormy was an Aries—all spontaneity and playful pushiness. If he tried to threaten Laddie's status, Laddie would promptly pin him to the ground by the neck to remind him who was boss, but never hurting his canine pal. Stormy would retreat . . . tail between his legs. Only rarely would Laddie react this way, and only if pushed.

"Another side of Scorpio Laddie is his very gentle and nurturing side. Laddie practically raised Stormy. As a puppy, Stormy would tease Laddie, and Laddie would simply take it in stride."

On September 4, Lori Jean received another dramatic sign of communication from Stormy.

"I was feeding liver bits to Laddie and Brandy, and each time that I would give them a piece of cooked liver, a large blue sphere of light would flash right next to them.

"After it had happened for the sixth time, I took a piece of liver and held it out to the spot where the light had been flashing. 'Here you go, Stormy,' I said.

"There were no more flashes of light after that. Of course Stormy's spirit did not take the piece of liver, but it was obvious that he remembered his favorite treat and that he still had an interest in it."

On November 19, Lori Jean faxed us with "something interesting" to report:

"The past two nights, while I have been in a relaxed state prior to sleep, I have heard a dog barking in our bedroom. It is not either Laddie or Brandy, who sleep in the room with us, but it is an etheric bark. I recognized that it was Stormy's bark, and today Spirit confirmed for me that it is he."

Lori Jean has been shown by her personal contact with angels on the other side that dogs progress into the Light just as we humans do.

"Caring angels meet them with peace and love. They stay for a time in the higher realms, and then God allows them to return to us in newer and healthier bodies. We've been told that Stormy will reincarnate and return to us in the spring of 1995."

How will you know if a dear departed dog has come back to you?

"They don't always come back," Lori Jean states, "but when you are meeting puppies, pay close attention and see if you recognize any distinctive personality traits that only you would know. They will give you telltale signs. You will know."

Lori Jean is saddened when she contemplates the sad truth that certain show dogs may be passed from home to home and never be valued as the spiritual individuals that they really are.

"Dogs are much more than their physical selves, just as we humans are. They are here to teach us about love. They are love. They are expressions of Divine Light, just as we are.

"You see, it matters not who we are, what we do, or what we own. It matters not what our beliefs are, or if we are white, brown, yellow, or black. The only thing that matters is love.

"Someday when we reach Heaven, we will not be asked what we owned, acquired, or accomplished. We will be asked how much, how often, and how deeply did we love.

"I believe that for dogs this question will be simple to answer—for they give love all the time."

Angels Guided Rebel and Gratis to the Other Side

Janie Howard of Upperco, Maryland, author of *Commune with the Angels,* shared her interspecies experiences with two dogs, Rebel and Gratis, and told how the angelic kingdom had aided her canine companions in their transition from physical life to a higher dimension.

Although she had grown up on her parents' farm with many dogs, Rebel, a schnauzer-poodle mix, a "schnoodle," was the first dog that was truly Janie's own. She had wonderful memories of glorious days spent on the farm with Rebel, swimming in the pond, running through meadows and fields.

Now, fifteen years later, poor Rebel had lost her hearing, was nearly blind, and had become quite lame.

At the same time that Janie was feeling great concern for the discomfort of her beloved dog, she was also undergoing the traumatic dissolution of her marriage.

On the fifteenth anniversary of Rebel's having come into Janie's life, fog shrouded the neighborhood. Janie had let Rebel outside; but then, when she had come to the door to let her "schnoodle" back in, she could not find her. Although Janie called Rebel's name for what seemed like hours, it was as though the dog had literally disappeared.

Since it was totally uncharacteristic of Rebel to wander away from home, Janie, who has property directly across from her parents' farm, enlisted their help in searching for the aged dog.

"The next morning, when the fog had lifted, my parents and I looked everywhere," Janie remembered. "We walked over fields and pastures calling for Rebel. I prayed to the angels for their help, but it appeared that she had simply vanished."

Janie tacked up notices and posters describing her lost pet. She contacted the Humane Society and placed newspaper ads.

At last a neighboring farmer telephoned her with the sad solution to the mystery of Rebel's disappearance.

She had apparently wandered to his place, about a mile away from Janie's property. She had appeared to the farmer to be staggering as she approached his farmyard. She wore no tags, because she never left Janie's or her parents' property.

The farmer claimed that because of Rebel's halting, staggering walk, he began to fear that she might be rabid. Concerned for the safety of his horses and cattle, he made the decision to destroy her without questioning any of the nearby neighbors to ascertain if anyone could identify the dog.

"I was devastated over the loss of my beloved companion," Janie said. "But I prayed to the angels to watch over Rebel, and I consoled myself with the knowledge that now that she was in spirit she would once again be able to run, to play, and to swim in a heavenly pond."

About a week later, Janie's former spouse learned of Rebel's death and called her office to express his sympathy.

"His call led to a profound healing for both of us, and we were able to have a conversation that would enable us to resolve the differences that we had begun to fear could only be settled in a courtroom.

"I was then able to perceive once again how wonderfully

all the kingdoms—angelic, human, and animal—work hand-in-hand to accomplish God's Divine Plan.

"My beloved Rebel, knowing how painful it would be for me to make the decision to put her to sleep in order to ease her pain and discomfort, had worked with the angels to bring about her own release. She was guided by the angels to a place where her death would be quick, and I could remain apart from it."

Janie had named her acreage Tulip-Poplar Hill, but now, in honor of the angels, she rechristened it Angel Heights, so Rebel could be buried in angelic ground.

"I was now down to one dog, Gratis, who was also getting up in years," she said. "I had had four bunnies, one dog, and one cat that had made their transition."

Some time later, Janie was at a party in Pittsburgh when a local intuitive of good reputation approached her and began to make polite conversation.

"He told me that he 'saw' a little dog around my feet. 'That's nice,' I smiled politely. "But then he went on to comment that he could not figure out why the little dog was wrapped in a Confederate flag.

" 'Please say nothing more,' I told him, visualizing my dear Rebel in my mind. 'You have just given me the greatest gift that you could possibly give me at this time.' "

When Janie Howard shared these stories with me in November of 1994, it had been only a week since her beloved dog Gratis had passed to the other side.

"Gratis had also been with me for fifteen years. She emanated great healing energy and always participated in my angelic attunement and healing sessions.

"Last Saturday, I was going out of town to conduct a seminar, and my parents would be coming by to look in on Gratis and to play with her.

"Just before I left, I suddenly felt inspired by Spirit to tell Gratis how important she was to me. At the same time, I inwardly heard the angels tell me that this would be the last time that I would see Gratis. I knew that she had been deteriorating physically, but defiantly I shouted, 'No! I will see her on Monday when I return.' "

While Janie was out of town, her parents found Gratis crying in pain. They got the veterinarian, who advised them the humane thing to do would be to put the dog to sleep. The dear Gratis died in the arms of Janie's "Earthangel" parents.

When she returned to find that her beloved Gratis was dead, Janie realized that Gratis had known, as had Rebel, that Janie would find it painfully difficult to make the final decision to put her to rest. Both dogs had spared her that major decision. Both of her blessed canine companions had worked with the angels to take that fateful step on their own.

"The incredible thing of it was, Gratis had chosen the *exact day and time* that Rebel had chosen to leave three years before. I know that Rebel had been waiting to show her the way.

"I *know* that the angels work with us," Janie affirmed as she concluded her moving testimony. "I *know* that the animals work with us. We are so blessed!"

Friendships are fragile things. Through human clumsiness we sometimes destroy even the very best of our relationships with others. If we humans could demonstrate the kind of unconditional love to one another that our canine companions show toward us, think of what a planet of peace and harmony we would inhabit.

If, as the Bible tells us, the Creator fashioned our kind just a little below the angels, were dogs created just a little below us?

But if, as the wise and holy teachers admonish us, to err is human and to forgive is divine, then it would often appear as though our dogs have moved a step or two ahead of us on the path of spiritual evolution.

It has always seemed to me that one of the greatest gifts that God has given us is the opportunity to establish a communications link with dogs, a species separate and unique from ourselves. We don't need to wait for a spaceship to land with an extraterrestrial crew to be able to attempt verbal or telephatic interaction. We have a marvelous, loving terrestrial species that has been standing by our side for the last 20,000 years, just waiting to bond with us, to blend with us, and to become one with us.

I have always respected dogs as sovereign entities, allied with us, yet different from us. I have tried never to denigrate them by regarding them as mere animated stuffed toys or living machines, nor have I sought to romanticize them as four-legged humans in fur coats.

When my children were small, I used to amuse them by grabbing hold of Reb, our beagle, and accusing him of being a little man in a dog costume. To the accompaniment of their delighted squeals of laughter, I would turn Reb over and run desperately probing fingers over his tummy while shouting: "All right, where's the zipper? I know you're not a dog! I know you're in there. Come out at once! The jig is up!"

The little game with Reb was funny because at times he seemed so humanlike; and yet, of course, he was not a human. He was a very intelligent, observant, loving, and completely charming dog.

If it is true that we learn our virtues from the friends who love us, then I would like to think that throughout my life my canine companions have taught me something of loyalty, devotion, integrity, patience, and love.

For me, the planet would be a very bleak place if it were

not for dogs. Indeed, God may have given us dogs to bless us, to make our present earth lives more tolerable, and to prepare us for the unconditional love that we are certain to find in Heaven.

References and Resources

Helping the Hurt and the Homeless

Doris Day, the famous singer-actress, left the recording studio and the silver screen to devote her energies exclusively to the assistance of dogs and other animals that are hungry, homeless, or hurt. Her foundation also provides dogs for adoption.

> The Doris Day Pet Foundation
> PO Box 8166
> Universal City, California 91608

Volunteering Your Dog As a Therapist

If you feel your dog is cheery, unflappable, eager to please, and patient—and if you really feel you want to share him or her with others—contact Therapy Dogs International or The Delta Society for information about how this might be accomplished.

Therapy Dogs International has certified about nine thousand dogs throughout the United States and Canada to provide comfort and companionship to the ill or the elderly.

> Therapy Dogs International
> 6 Hilltop Road
> Mendham, New Jersey 07945
> 201-543-0888

The Delta Society has certified about one thousand canines through its Pet Partners program.

> The Delta Society
> PO Box 1080
> Renton, Washington 98057-9906
> 206-226-7357

By contacting Canine Companions for Independence, you can learn how you may be able to raise a dog from puppyhood so that it might be trained to assist people with special needs.

Call 800-767-BARK

Animal/Human Communication

Penelope Smith offers *Species Link,* a quarterly journal, as well as numerous books and tapes. She also travels the United States, Canada and abroad presenting lectures and workshops dealing with interspecies communication. For a free catalog, write to:

Pegasus Publications
PO Box 1060
Point Reyes, California 94956
Or call 415-663-1247

To order books or tapes with your credit card from either the U.S. or Canada, call 800-356-9315

Spiritually Inspired Works Containing References to Dogs

Beverly Hale Watson has authored a number of lovely spiritually inspired books of poetry and prose. She also has special talents regarding dogs and other animals which have been employed with great success by Humane Societies.

Sevenfold Peace Foundation
4704 Quail Ridge Drive
Charlotte, North Carolina 28227
704-545-8042

Sandra J. Radhoff's book, *The Kyrian Letters: Transformative Messages for Higher Vision,* contains messages devoted to dogs and other pets and the spiritual energies contained within the animal kingdom.

Heritage Publications
PO Box 444
Virginia Beach, Virginia 23458
800-862-2923

Unusual Talents and Abilities of Dogs

Strange Powers of Pets, a Literary Guild selection by Brad Steiger and Sherry Hansen Steiger, explores the mysterious psychic dimension that we share with canines and other animals—incredible sagas of dogs that found their way home against impossible odds; dogs that rescued their human families; ghost dogs that returned to say goodbye; and dozens of other incredible accounts.

Strange Powers of Pets and its exciting sequel, *More Strange Powers of Pets,* are both published in illustrated, hardcover editions by Donald I. Fine and may be ordered by calling 800–253–6476.

Accounts of Canine Survival After Death

Scott S. Smith's well-documented book, *Pet Souls: Evidence that Animals Survive Death,* is published by:

Light Source Research
2455 Calle Roble
Thousand Oaks, California 91360
805–497–4950

Angelic Kingdoms and Canines

Janie Howard, author of *Commune with the Angels,* conducts workshops and hosts an annual Angel Conference. She also publishes a newsletter and is available for private consultations.

Janie Howard
PO Box 95
Upperco, Maryland 21155
410–833–6912   Fax: 410–526–0399

Lori Jean and Charles Flory publish *The Enchanted Spirits Newsletter.* Lori Jean is available for private consultations, and Charles will provide a personal astrological chart for your canine.

Lori Jean and Charles Flory
PO Box 1328
Conifer, Colorado 80433
303–838–1977

Kimberly Marooney has recently created *Angel Blessings, Cards of Sacred Guidance and Inspiration.*

Merill West Publishing
PO Box 1227
Carmel, California 93921
800–676–1256

Angels Over Their Shoulders: Children's Encounters with Heavenly Beings, by Brad Steiger and Sherry Hansen Steiger, has chapters exploring the interaction between pets, angels, and children. A Fawcett-Columbine book. Call 800–733–3000.

Sherry Hansen Steiger creates imaginative, handcrafted animal angels, delightful winged and gowned dogs, and other animals that she calls her "Ark Angels." For an illustrated brochure, send $1.00 and a stamped, self-addressed #10 envelope to:

Sherry Hansen Steiger
PO Box 434
Forest City, Iowa 50436

For further information concerning Grandmother Twylah's teachings of the Seneca, write to:

The Seneca Historical Society
Cattaraugus Reservation
12199 Brant Reservation Road
Irving, New York 14081